Books by Sibéal Pounder

Bad Mermaids
Bad Mermaids: On the Rocks

Witch Wars
Witch Switch
Witch Watch
Witch Glitch
Witch Snitch

BAD
Mermaids
On the Rocks

SIBÉAL POUNDER

Illustrated by
Jason Cockcroft

BLOOMSBURY
CHILDREN'S BOOKS
LONDON OXFORD NEW YORK NEW DELHI SYDNEY

BLOOMSBURY CHILDREN'S BOOKS
Bloomsbury Publishing Plc
50 Bedford Square, London WC1B 3DP, UK

BLOOMSBURY, BLOOMSBURY CHILDREN'S BOOKS and the Diana logo
are trademarks of Bloomsbury Publishing Plc

First published in Great Britain in 2018 by Bloomsbury Publishing Plc

A catalogue record for this book is available from the British Library

ISBN: PB: 978-1-4088-7714-2; eBook: 978-1-4088-7715-9

2 4 6 8 10 9 7 5 3 1

Typeset by RefineCatch Limited, Bungay, Suffolk
Printed and bound in Great Britain by CPI Group (UK) Ltd, Croydon CR0 4YY

MIX
Paper from
responsible sources
FSC® C020471

To find out more about our authors and books visit www.bloomsbury.com
and sign up for our newsletters

For Frankie! A truly fabulous writer,
reader and mermaid

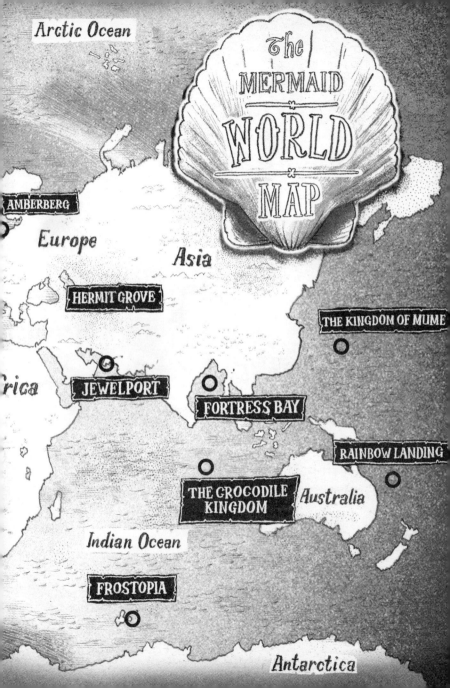

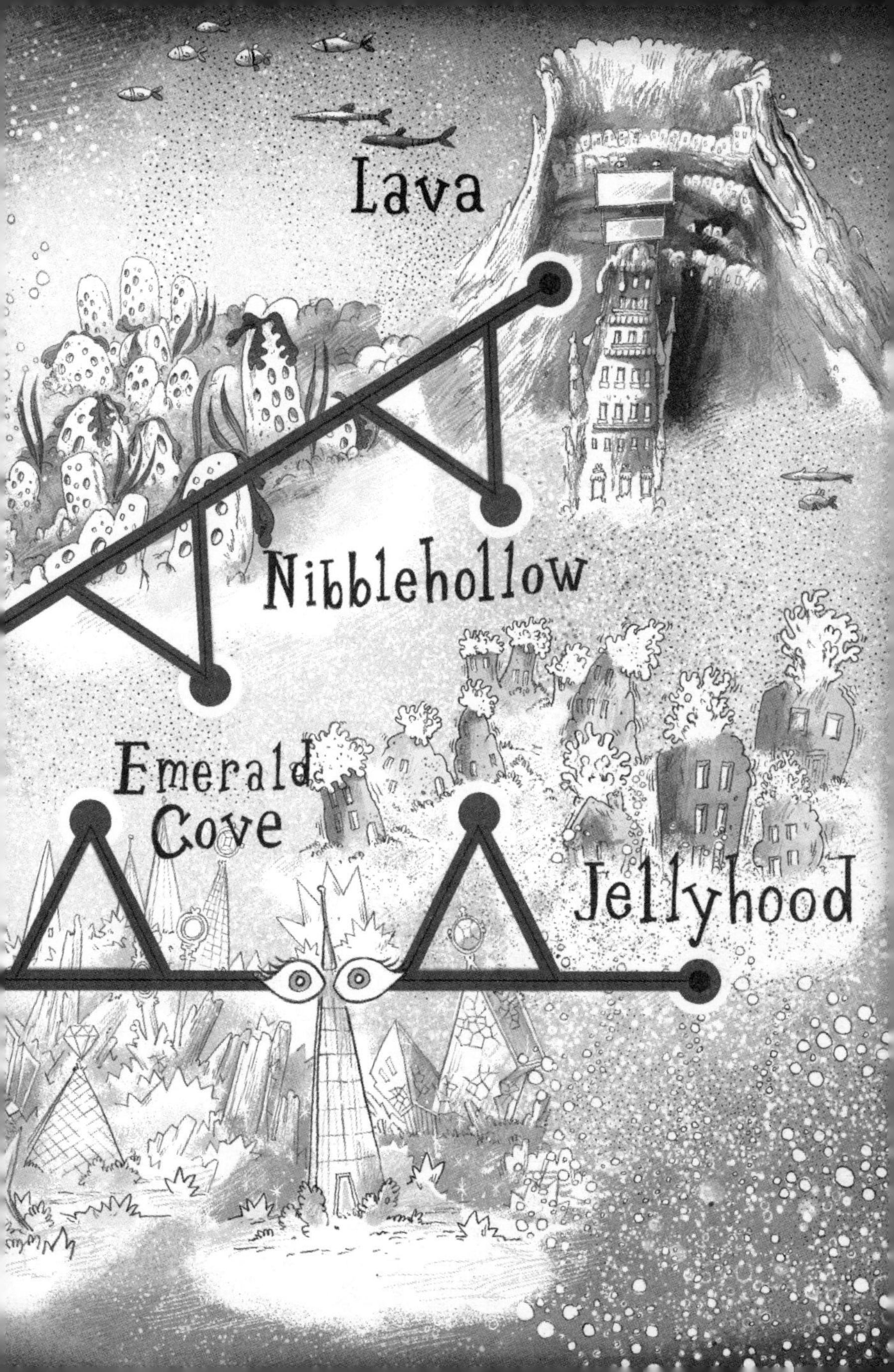
Lava
Nibblehollow
Emerald Cove
Jellyhood

The Story So Far ...

Last time in mermaid-filled waters, Beattie, Mimi and Zelda thwarted the plot of one seriously bad mermaid, and did a lot of driving in a *technically* stolen clam car.

But they failed to notice a very important thing - a small, human-shaped detail, right at the very beginning.

Maybe you remember?

There was a girl standing at the ice-cream stall as they raced to the beach to pick up a crabagram. The girl with the claw-shaped hand, bent forever from constantly holding ice-cream cones? The one with the smile and swirls of sunburn on her face? Well, her name is Paris, and it is of the utmost importance that she meets Beattie, Mimi and Zelda.

But there's a problem - Paris is a human on land, and when we left Beattie, Mimi and Zelda they were trapped on a sunken ship called the *Merry Mary*, hurtling through the Upper Realms. They couldn't be further away from each other. Paris is about to open up her ice-cream stall for the day, and Beattie, Mimi and Zelda are about to discover that the mermaid world is a lot bigger than just their Hidden Lagoon.

And they are also about to discover that seahorses can get seasick.

But that's not important.

1

Would You Rather...?

The *Merry Mary* sailed sideways through a hefty hulk of firefly squid. They danced around the old ship, illuminating it with their bright blue lights. Those squid had no idea just who was trapped inside.

'Would you rather,' Zelda said, slapping her tail against one of the ship's portholes, 'have a tail that shouted insults at you every hour for the rest of your life, or be followed around by a tiny troop of sea slugs?'

Hilma stuck her nose in the air. 'I've already told you, Zelda. I'm not going to answer your silly, pointless questions.'

'But if you had to choose,' Zelda pressed.

Hilma angrily crossed her arms and said quietly, 'Probably the sea slugs.'

Zelda shook her head disapprovingly. 'They'd slime all over your favourite hats, Hilma. They'd slime.'

At the other side of the boat's main cabin, Mimi, Zelda's twin, sat by the window, her nose pressed against a porthole and her multicoloured tail curled upward like a table. On it sat a pair of false teeth.

'There's got to be a way out!' Beattie shouted as she swam fast into the cabin. She'd searched all over for an exit – every corridor, every cupboard and door on the old sunken ship. 'It's completely on lockdown. Can you tell where we are yet?'

Mimi wiped her nose across the window, making a slightly wet smudge. 'Um … no.'

Beattie flopped down next to her and grabbed the false teeth. 'Steve,' she said as she opened them. A tiny trail of seahorse sick floated out, followed by a seahorse wearing a mermaid cone top.

'Excuse you!' he said, then threw up again.

Steve was the only seahorse in the whole lagoon

4

that could speak. No one knew why. He slept in the false teeth.

Beattie leaned back to avoid the tiny trail of seahorse sick. 'Are you seasick, Steve? I know we're on a boat – but we *are* still underwater ...'

'Can seahorses even get seasick?' Zelda said as the trail of sick made its way past her. 'Ignore me,' she said as she watched it go. 'Steve has thrown up some evidence.'

'We're never getting off this ship,' Beattie said, stroking Steve's back. 'We're well and truly trapped.'

'Beattie,' Zelda said quietly, 'would you rather ... have one of Hilma's hats stuck to your face forever or –'

'STOP ASKING THE POINTLESS QUESTIONS!' Hilma roared. 'They're stupid. And always vaguely offensive about me.'

The boat tipped, sending Hilma and Zelda sliding at speed across the cabin. They splatted into Beattie and Mimi.

'Oh look,' Mimi said casually, her face smooshed against the window. 'There's something out there.'

 5

Beattie pushed her to the side and peered out. It was dark, apart from the occasional flash of luminous blue from the firefly squid, and a strange green glow, just beneath them in a rocky canyon covered in coral.

'What is that green thing?' Hilma said, pointing at it, her finger shaking slightly.

Beattie squinted and wiped the window. As they got closer, she could see the green glow was coming from the eyes of a large stone carved into the shape of a crocodile.

The *Merry Mary* dived into the canyon.

The crocodile statue's eyes began flashing.

'No way,' Zelda said. 'It's communicating with the ship.'

'Don't be ridiculous,' Beattie said.

'It might be a human device to trap us!' Hilma wailed. 'Humans are evil you know! They have toes! TOES!'

Beattie's tail shook as the ship was sucked downward, sinking fast. It connected with the stone crocodile with a strange clang.

Hilma whimpered as an emerald light engulfed them. 'The toes are coming,' she choked.

Zelda slapped her with her tail. 'It's not a horror film, Hilma, calm down.'

 7

The ship started spinning. Then came a groaning sound and everything started to rumble.

'I don't like this!' Beattie shouted as Steve dived back into his false teeth.

'WHOA! Look at that!' Zelda cried.

In the side of the canyon the coral fell away, revealing a giant cave entrance, at least ten times the size of the ship.

'Toes,' Hilma said, sounding defeated.

'No human made this,' Mimi whispered, as their ship glided towards the rock opening and disappeared inside.

2

Everyone, Meet Paris...

Paris smiled as she handed an ice cream to a kid with baggy swim shorts and grabby hands.

Behind her a large factory loomed.

The kid licked the ice cream. 'Why do you work at an ice-cream stall?'

'To make money to buy parts for my inventions,' Paris said.

'But my daddy says your family own that Silkensocks sock factory right there.' He pointed a chubby finger at the factory behind Paris. 'So you're really rich.'

Paris leaned forward and whispered. 'I like to keep my inventions secret. If I had to ask my mother for the money, she would want to know what it was for.'

The little boy considered her answer for a moment

and then nodded in approval. 'What inventions have you made?'

'Well,' Paris said, picking up the chocolate shavings and sprinkling some on the boy's ice cream, 'lots of things. I like to call myself the GADGET QUEEN.' She laughed.

The boy didn't.

'Are they any good, your inventions?' he asked.

'Oh yes,' Paris lied. Most of her inventions tended to fall apart. 'Almost all my inventions have been a huge sockcess!'

'Success,' the little boy said.

'Yes, that's what I said.'

'No,' he said. 'You said *sock*cess.'

Paris groaned. 'It's a habit. I tend to say sock by accident. A lot.'

'Where are your inventions?' he asked.

'The older ones are in bits in my bedroom cupboard, up there.' She turned and pointed at a sock-shaped tower in the northern wing of the factory. 'But my finest invention, well, you're looking at it.'

The boy's eyes lit up. 'You invented ICE CREAM?'

Paris burst out laughing. 'I *wish*.' She slapped the ice-cream stall. 'No, this is my secret den. This is GADGET QUEEN HEADQUARTERS.'

The little boy looked unimpressed.

'It's just a stall.'

'That's what I wanted it to look like,' Paris said with a knowing smile.

The little boy didn't look convinced.

An old woman walked past with a crab wrapped up snugly in a Silkensocks sock.

'Rock-a-bye, crabby, in a small sock, when the wind blows the socky will … sock,' the old woman sang.

'That was weird,' Paris said, then turned back to the little boy.

'One more thing,' he said. 'Please could you ask them to change the Silkensocks socks TV advert. It's horrible.'

Paris watched as he tottered off. The advert had been the same for years – and it was terrifying. Her mother's voice sang, grandly, 'TOES DESERVE SILKENSOCKS,' and then some toes danced across the screen, all singing, 'TOES DESERVE SILKEN-SOCKS.' It finished with a giant sock gobbling them up.

It was her mother's idea. And if you knew Paris's mother, you'd know that was exactly the kind of thing that went on in her brain.

Paris smiled as people walked past, waiting until the coast was clear. She fiddled impatiently with her hair, which she'd pulled into a chunky plait that practically reached her waist. It was time she checked on her latest invention.

A large family, all arguing and chatting loudly over each other, strode past. Paris took her chance. Glancing from left to right, she readjusted her knee-high socks, and as the family blocked the view of the ice-cream stall, she flipped open the fake ice-cream cone on the side and pressed a button. There was a click, and she was gone.

But she hadn't gone far. Hidden under the ice-cream stall was Paris's high-tech den. It was submerged in the sea, with glass walls that gave her a clear view out into the ocean. A crab scuttled towards the glass, looking at her suspiciously as she fiddled with screens and little bits of half-made gadgets. She pulled on a pair of clam-shell headphones, which she used to listen to conversations on the beach, and pushed papers off the control panel, revealing a high-tech tracking system decorated with ice-cream stickers.

Three dots flashed on it – one purple, one green and one with multicoloured stripes.

The tracking devices she'd placed on Beattie, Mimi and Zelda were working! She punched the air in victory.

'Hang on a sockond – I mean second,' she said. She took off her headphones and turned to the crab. 'The mermaids are out in the Atlantic Ocean! Their home is a place called the Hidden Lagoon. And that's in the Pacific Ocean. Why would they be in the Atlantic?'

The crab stared at her as if to say, *You know I don't talk, yes?*

Paris leapt to her feet.

'Wait a SOCKOND!' she cried. 'Oh wow, I think I might know ...' She rifled frantically through the papers on her desk and pulled out an old book titled *IT HAD A TAIL (Stop Calling Me a Liar)*. Her mother had written it when she was young and it was full of mermaid research. She'd spent *a lot* of money finding mermaid things – ancient shell tops and seaweed letters – but she'd never found a hidden mermaid kingdom. She had lots of theories about where they were though.

'THAT'S IT!' Paris shouted, startling the crab. He slipped off the rock. 'There's a kingdom where the mermaids have crocodile tails and the water is emerald green.' She turned the book around to show the crab a doodle of a mermaid with a crocodile-skin tail. 'And it's hidden somewhere in the *Atlantic*.'

She grabbed a map and placed it over the tracking screen. Carefully she traced the spot where the three mermaids were. She scrawled 'THE CROCODILE KINGDOM?' next to it.

'I'm a genius!' she cried. 'Gadget Queen strikes again!'

She held the map up and smiled at it.

An alarm sounded and she fell off her chair with a bang.

'Ow,' Paris groaned from under her desk.

The alarm sounded again. 'All right, all right, Susan Cam,' she said through gritted teeth.

Tacked to the wall was a large screen, decorated with fuzzy spotted socks hanging like bunting. A huge red light was flashing above it.

'I planted a tiny camera in my mother's hair,' Paris informed the crab. 'It sounds the alarm when she's close by and shows me a view from her head. Look, she's walking towards us. I'd better go!'

She hit the button on her chair. In a flash she was back at the stall like she'd never left.

'Paris, my disappointing sock,' her mother sniped. Susan was wearing her trademark spotted socks and stilettos and a face so angry the inflatable pool toys on the stall next door had deflated. 'Are you listening, Paris?'

Paris casually poured some sprinkles over the ice cream. 'Uh-huh?'

 16

'We're releasing the crabs. We need to clear the beach so no one grows suspicious.'

Paris raised an eyebrow. 'What crabs? Why would you –'

'FREE ICE CREAM!' her mother began shouting. 'FREE ICE CREAM COURTESY OF THE SILKENSOCKS!'

There was a ripple of excitement on the beach, followed by a flurry of sand and swimsuits.

'Distract them,' her mother ordered as she tottered off towards the emptying beach.

The rumble of bare feet and flip-flops grew louder.

Paris held her breath as everyone lunged for the ice-cream stall.

 17

3

On the Rocks

When the ship ground to a halt, it sounded like someone had turned the volume up. The rumble of chattering mermaids dribbled through the ship, until Beattie could barely hear the panicked wheeze-breathing Hilma was doing.

'Who is that chattering?' Zelda said.

'Toes,' Hilma whimpered knowingly. 'It's the toes.'

Mimi put a hand on Hilma's elaborately decorated shoulder. 'Toes don't speak. Or at least, have never spoken in front of anyone. You know, I don't think they have mouths, actually ...'

A strange green glow engulfed the ship and the portholes popped open.

'What was that?' Hilma said with a jump.

'How strange,' Beattie said, gripping the edge of the porthole and peeking out. Through the bubbles she could make out crowds of mermaids – hundreds of them – dressed oddly and entirely in shades of green. All of them had flamboyant shoulder pads.

Zelda swam up over Beattie and pushed her head aside to get a better look. 'Oh look at the shoulder pads. You'll fit right in here, Hilma!'

Beattie squeezed her face back in beside Zelda's for another look. They were at some sort of port. A wonky line of impressive sunken vessels stretched off into the distance.

'Where do you think we are?' Zelda asked.

A crocodile swam past.

Then another.

Beattie's mouth fell open.

The crocodiles. The weirdly dressed mermaids.

'Um, Beattie?' Zelda said, sticking her finger in and out of Beattie's gaping mouth.

'THE GREEN EVERYTHING!' Beattie cried.

'Yes, Beattie,' Zelda said slowly. 'Green.'

 19

'The Crocodile Kingdom,' she spluttered. 'I think we're in the Crocodile Kingdom!'

'The Crocodile Kingdom isn't *real*, Beattie,' Hilma scoffed. 'That's just something your mother believes in. And everyone knows she's insane.'

Beattie's mum was the travel reporter for *Clamzine* back in the Hidden Lagoon. She was a gutsy explorer, currently swimming the Upper Realms and searching for hidden mermaid kingdoms, though most mermaids thought they were entirely mythical.

'Wait,' Zelda said. 'I thought crocodiles need to surface to breathe?'

'They say the water within the walls of the Crocodile Kingdom is laced with magic,' Beattie explained. 'The crocodiles never have to leave.' Her tail flopped. 'Wait, if we *are* in the Crocodile Kingdom, then that means no one will find us here. No one believes this place exists! Well, apart from my mum, but the chances of her finding it and getting inside are about as likely as Hilma saying something positive.'

21

'It's *not* the Crocodile Kingdom,' Hilma said. 'Someone made the place up years ago, and silly mermaids like you have believed it ever since.'

'I'm going to get a better look,' Beattie said. 'There's no point hiding in here, waiting for someone to save us. I'll have to find a way to get us home.'

'We're not letting you go alone,' Mimi said.

'We're DEFINITELY coming too,' Zelda said, brandishing a fist.

Hilma frantically waved goodbye. 'Have THE BEST time, you three!'

Zelda narrowed her eyes at Hilma. 'You have no guts.'

Mimi shook her head. 'Everyone has guts.' She patted Hilma's belly. 'Yep, there they are.'

Hilma shoved Mimi's hand away. 'I'm not going to go out there.'

Steve popped out of his false teeth and nestled into Beattie's hair.

'Even Steve is coming with us,' Zelda said. 'And he's a seahorse.'

He poked his nose out of Beattie's hair. 'I'm a *MIRACLE*.'

'Yeah, yeah,' Zelda grumbled, pulling herself up to one of the portholes.

'We'll be back soon, Hilma,' Beattie said. 'Stay put. Don't go anywhere.'

Hilma stuck her nose in the air and crossed her arms. 'Obviously I'm going to stay put.'

Beattie nodded, and the three of them squeezed out of the porthole with a pop.

'WAIT!' Hilma cried. 'You forgot your false teeth!'

But the others were already outside and didn't hear her.

The false teeth floated slowly past Hilma's face.

She prodded them with her finger and gagged. 'Eugh, *yuck.*'

MARITZA MIST'S
WATER WITCH CATALOGUE

MERMAID DUPLICATION!
Double trouble or DOUBLE THE FUN?

Inspired by the water witches of Octopolli
and their sublime potion-mixing skills,
one sprinkle of this little powder will
make two of you. Yes, that's right!
Create another you in minutes.*

*Due to a slight quantity error when mixing this potion,
your duplicate is likely to shout 'FISH EYE!' every now
and again. Apologies for any inconvenience caused.

4

Jellywich! Ringletti! Icetipple!

'What a weird old ship,' Mimi said with a smile. 'Why in all watery bits has it taken us to the Crocodile Kingdom?'

Beattie looked up at the grand old ship. 'Look, on the flag! It's a crocodile! The *Merry Mary* must be from here – the ship sailed home!'

'The *Merry Mary* belonged to Mary Ruster, the mermaid queen who lived hundreds of years ago in the Hidden Lagoon,' Zelda said. 'How would she have a ship from the Crocodile Kingdom? And how did it make it all the way to our lagoon?'

Mimi nodded thoughtfully. 'She must've visited the Crocodile Kingdom and brought it back with her as a souvenir.'

'A *souvenir*?' Zelda said. 'Mimi, last time you went

on a trip you brought me back a rock with "Zizzle" carved on it.'

'They didn't have one that said "Zelda",' Mimi chirped.

'Will you two shush and look at this place!' Beattie said, spinning them both round.

Ships were pulling into bays and mermaids in the most fabulous green outfits were unloading chests of jewels and shells and lace-patterned reams of seaweed.

'Oh! The new clothes fabrics from Jewelport!' one of the mermaids cheered. 'Gimme.'

'Jewelport?' Zelda said, an eyebrow raised. 'I've never heard of it.'

Beattie turned to the twins. 'It must be another place we've never ...' She trailed off. 'Your hair!' she cried. 'It's turning green!'

'My hair is always green,' Zelda said. She turned and pointed at Beattie. 'Wait, but *yours* isn't purple any more!'

Beattie caught a glimpse of her hair in a mirrored trunk. She somersaulted backwards when she noticed the tail of the mermaid carrying it.

'Crocodile-patterned tails,' she whispered to Zelda and Mimi. 'This *proves* it. We're in the Crocodile Kingdom.'

'It could be a coincidence,' Zelda said. 'Us being in the Crocodile Kingdom is as likely as a talking parrot.'

'Zelda,' Beattie said firmly. 'Parrots *can* talk. And I thought you said you were going to stop using human words.'

'Calm down, you microwave with eyes,' Zelda said with a smug smile.

Beattie groaned.

'You love me really, Beattie,' Zelda said, swimming over her head. 'Come on, I thought we were exploring!'

The three of them swam slowly down the dock, past a group of takeaway food stalls carved into the rock. All along the swimway were flashing neon signs in blinding green:

FRESH JELLYWICH FROM JEWELPORT!
RINGLETTI JUST IN FROM OCTOPOLLI!
ICETIPPLE ALL THE WAY FROM FROSTOPIA!

Mermaids were clustered in large groups around the stalls, elbowing each other and grabbing food.

One threw a huge ice barrel into the Frostopia food stall.

'Where's the rest of it?!' the mermaid behind the counter shouted.

'You're going to have to pay me extra for that one alone,' the other mermaid scoffed, swimming fast back to his sunken ship. 'You try getting into Frostopia! I had to outswim a pod of security whales on the outer ice walls just to get that one!'

'It's real,' Beattie grinned, leaning against the Jellywich stall to steady herself. 'The Crocodile Kingdom, Octopolli, other mermaid cities we never even knew about, they're all *real*. It's not just us out there in the Hidden Lagoon. There are millions of us *all over the world*. Just like my mum has been trying to tell everyone for years!'

'No. I know what this is,' Zelda said. 'We're dead.' She flopped on to a rock. 'This is obviously what death is. Some weird mermaid place where Beattie and her mum are correct about everything.'

'We're not dead,' Mimi said, taking a bite out of a bright green jelly sandwich. 'I'm eating a sandwich!'

'How are we going to find a way home?' Beattie said quietly as she watched mermaids swim in single file on to a ship. They all had large shell suitcases.

'Make the most of your holiday in Pinkly Lagoon with these top tips!' a mermaid handing out seaweed flyers shouted.

'It's not like we can get back on that old bathtub,'

Zelda said, gesturing towards the *Merry Mary*, just as its mast fell off with a bang.

'No,' Beattie said glumly. 'We'll have to sneak on to another one.'

The boat going to Pinkly Lagoon began flashing a luminous green colour.

'Why is it doing that?' Zelda shouted, holding her arm up to shield her eyes.

'It's Upper Realm glue,' the mermaid behind the Ringletti stand said, her curls wafting in the water.

'What's Upper Realm glue?' Zelda asked as the ship stopped glowing.

'They cover the boats in it, so when the boat is in Upper Realm territory, where the *humans* lurk, it's completely sealed – no way in and no way out, for safety. Doors and portholes only open when the ship docks back in the Lower Realms, in safe mermaid territory. Why don't you know about Upper Realm glue?'

The three of them stood there blinking, then Beattie started fake laughing. 'Oh, ha! Ha! ... ha. Yes, I remember now! I'd forgotten! Obviously! Yes ...'

 30

The Ringletti stall mermaid looked at them strangely, and then got back to scooping Ringletti rings into serving shells.

'Great,' Beattie mumbled. 'So even if we did sneak on to a ship, we wouldn't be able to get off until we got to the destination, which would just be another mermaid place no one in the Hidden Lagoon believes in or knows about. We'd be in exactly the same position we are now.'

'We'll find another way,' Mimi said, biting into her Jellywich. 'It's *us*.'

At the stall next to them, a strange mermaid dropped her shell full of Ringletti and gawped at them. 'Water witches,' she whispered, her eyes fixed on Beattie, Mimi and Zelda, but her head moving slightly to the left so some of the Ringletti she'd dropped could float into her open mouth. She chewed it quickly. '*Water witches*.'

Steve popped out of Beattie's hair. 'WHERE'S MY BEDROOM?'

The three of them looked at each other.

Steve closed his eyes. 'You *left* my *bedroom* on the *sunken ship*,' he said faintly.

 31

'Oh no, we forgot the false teeth,' Zelda said flatly. 'Whatever will we do?'

'We need to go back and get MY BEDROOM!' Steve squealed.

They didn't notice but at that moment the strange mermaid pulled out a little sachet shaped like a fish. She tore it open and squeezed out some gloopy liquid, running her fingers through it as it wafted away.

There was a snapping sound and the false teeth appeared in her hand. She grinned and held them up. 'The perfect way to introduce myself.'

'No one is stopping you from going to get your false teeth,' Zelda said, sneakily trying to take a bite of Mimi's Jellywich.

'My body is TINY!' Steve scoffed. 'I couldn't possibly swim that far.'

The strange mermaid plonked the false teeth down on the stall in front of them.

They all stared at them.

'Oh,' Steve said. 'My bedroom.'

'You, and you, and you, and YOU,' the strange

32

mermaid said, pointing a finger at Steve, 'are welcome.'

'The teeth,' Beattie said. She picked them up to make sure they were really Steve's. 'How did you get them? And … who are you?'

The strange mermaid smiled. 'I'm a water witch.' She looked around to check no one was listening. 'Just like *you*.'

5

Socks and Crabs

Back in her bedroom at the sock-shaped stone tower Paris face-planted on her grand four-poster bed.

'Oh limp little sock, you were very useful distracting the beach fools with the free ice cream,' she heard her mother say from the doorway.

Paris mumbled a 'No problem'.

She heard the tinkling sound of stilettos on the floor.

'You've really helped with my plan to convert our sock factory.'

'Convert it into what? A shoe factory?' Paris mumbled into the covers.

'No, silly socky – it will soon be *Mermaid World*.'

Paris rolled over so she was staring up at her mother. 'Mermaid World?'

'No one will expect us to turn a sock factory into the

number one destination for viewing *real* mermaids, because mermaids don't have feet. And socks are for feet,' Susan explained.

'I get it,' Paris said.

'Everyone is going to go wild! We'll be the talk of the world! We'll be famous.'

'Infamous,' Paris said.

'Well, that word has more letters so it's probably even better.'

'It's not,' Paris said. 'Hang on … what's that got to do

with releasing crabs on the beach?'

'I need to fish for some mermaids. According to my research, they use crabs to communicate. So I dumped a load of crabs with messages into the ocean. But I don't know how their crab system works exactly. I've been sending a crab with every sock mail order. Millions of sock customers have opened their sock package and found a crab, which they will have thrown outside. And each crab will have made its way to the nearest sea!'

'You've been sending crabs in the post?' Paris said flatly. 'Wait, is that why I saw an old woman with a crab in a sock earlier?'

Susan Silkensocks beamed proudly. 'It's a foolproof plan.' She leaned down to pull up one of her spotted socks. 'Whip up the waters to catch a fish, is how the saying goes. My crabs are going to spread rumours, fake information. Soon everyone will be fighting among themselves – it'll be chaos – and *that's* when I'll go fishing. I've already got one, you know.'

'A *mermaid*?' Paris spluttered.

Susan Silkensocks squealed and threw her favourite

shell box up in the air. She caught it triumphantly. 'A *REAL* MERMAID.'

Paris eyed the box like it was an evil little sibling. Her mother never went anywhere without it.

Susan Silkensocks beamed at the thing. It was grubby and old with a giant 'F' engraved on it.

'This is how I always knew mermaids were real!' Susan Silkensocks said, gripping the box tightly. 'Of course, no one believed me all those years ago. I leapt out at a mermaid and she dropped it. Oh, it had shimmering paste in it that looked like a glorious, liquefied mermaid tail! And then one day, *you* ate it.'

Paris rolled her eyes. She'd heard the story a million times. She'd been punished for eating it a million more.

'This box means more to me than anything. More than even *you*, Paris,' her mother sneered.

'So … you just mentioned you caught a mermaid? Where did you put it?' Paris asked, trying to casually slip it into the conversation without sounding too desperate to know.

'I put her in a tank in the factory!'

 37

Paris shook her head. 'You are *such* a cliché.'

'I'm fabulously unique,' Susan Silkensocks spat. 'I'm wearing spotted socks and stilettos for goodness' sake!'

Paris smooshed her face back into the covers as Susan Silkensocks stomped out of the door and down the corridor. As soon as the footsteps had faded, Paris leapt to her feet and grabbed her backpack covered in mermaid doodles. 'I'd better get to work,' she said with a determined nod – and with that, she climbed out of her bedroom window.

MARITZA MIST'S
WATER WITCH CATALOGUE

SECRET'S OUT

Ever wanted to know another mermaid's
secrets? Or are you keen to find out some juicy
gossip? With this secret-shouting fish, you can
discover something about a mermaid that
they'd rather keep secret.

INSTRUCTIONS: Remove the fish carefully
from the box and rub it on the head of the mermaid
you'd like to know a secret about. After
rubbing the fish on the mermaid's head, place
the fish in the palm of your hand and wait.
If done properly, the fish should shout the secret,
and then swim away.

WARNING: As per new Water Witch Council rules,
and so that this spell is not misused, the fish will also shout
one of your secrets, so it is fair. We discourage mean
spells and suggest mermaids only use this spell in
special circumstances.

6

Gadget Queen Strikes Again

It was pitch-black inside the Silkensocks Factory and Paris only had an old torch from her backpack. It flickered as she sneaked in and spun down the corridor, stopping when she reached the SOCK STOCK room. It was the biggest room in the factory, and the one that led out on to the pier.

If her mother was telling the truth, this was where the mermaid would be. It was closest to the sea, so easy to sneak a mermaid in after dark. Plus there were hundreds of boxes and stacks of socks everywhere: it would be easy to hide a tank.

She pushed the doors open and fell backwards.

A giant sparkly sign that read *MERMAID WORLD* swung overhead. Instead of the floor-to-ceiling boxes of socks, there were huge tanks, and a bar with *FOAM*

40

SHAKES written on the sign above it. A massive poster of Clippee – a lobster wearing a dress – hung next to a huge fake shark that was suspended in the air. The writing on it said *JAWELLA'S RESTAURANT THIS WAY* with an arrow pointing into the shark's mouth. Paris walked slowly to the middle of the room. There was a huge empty space. She shone the torch on the little sign on the floor.

Genuine mermaid buildings dug up from the deep!

'Oh SOCK!' Paris cried. 'She's not just going to fish out mermaids – she's going to dig the place up!'

She hastily dropped to her knees and ripped her backpack open. She needed to find that mermaid and free her. She could swim back to the Hidden Lagoon and warn them all – they'd be prepared for a horrible Susan Silkensocks invasion. They'd thwart her plans! Quickly, she rifled around and pulled out a small shell, flipping it open to reveal a dial with a picture of a mermaid and a picture of a human. She pointed it at herself and a light came on next to the picture of the human.

She stood up and pointed it around the room.

The lights on the dial flickered.

Nothing.

Nothing.

Nothing.

She shook it slightly. Maybe it was broken. Or maybe there wasn't a mermaid in there. Maybe her mother had made it up. That would be a very Susan thing to do ...

Was that a *squeak*?

Paris turned around slowly. There, floating in a tiny tank and tucked into the shadows, was the most beautiful mermaid she had ever seen. She was fast asleep, her face smooshed against the glass, with an assortment of dribble strands decorating her chin.

She also had the wrinkliest hand Paris had ever seen.

The mermaid snorted herself awake and barely blinked when she saw Paris staring at her hand. 'Stagnant water does that to us. The Silkensocks human who fishnapped me hasn't changed the water since I got here.'

'That's OK,' Paris said, holding up her claw hand. 'Mine is forever bent from constantly holding ice-cream cones.'

They high-fived. Paris grinned. Ever since she was little, she'd watched mermaids emerging on the beach for their summer on land with legs. It was so obvious to her and she could never understand why the humans didn't notice them. But Paris wasn't like most humans – she spotted things others were too busy to see.

'I'm Arabella Cod, Queen of the Hidden Lagoon,' the mermaid said.

'Nice to meet you,' Paris said. 'I'm Paris, worker at the ice-cream stall and Gadget Queen.'

'It's nice to meet another royal,' Arabella Cod said.

Paris swallowed loudly. 'Well … I'm not exactly *roy–*'

'Can you help me escape?' Arabella Cod asked. 'I'll reward you.'

'No need for a reward,' Paris said. 'I'll gladly thwart my mother's evil plans for free.'

She pulled a couple of large shoeboxes from her backpack and stuck them on either side of the tank. Arabella Cod leaned out to take a look just as a pair of mannequin legs popped out of the boxes and found their feet on the floor. The tank wobbled and rose up high as the legs made their way towards the factory doors. Arabella Cod grabbed a foam shake on the way past the bar. She spat it out instantly.

'Oh cods, this is *not* the recipe. You know that horrible woman who fishnapped me said mermaid food sounded DISGUSTING. She's obviously made some horrible human equivalent!'

'She's a fussy eater,' Paris said as she heaved the heavy factory door open, revealing a short pier and the inky sea beyond. 'After you.'

There was a bang at the other end of the factory – followed by the horribly familiar sound of skipping stilettos.

'She's here,' Paris said, her eyes wide. She hastily closed the factory door and raced over to the slow-moving tank.

Arabella Cod leaned out and stared at the legs. 'Can't you make them go faster?'

'Probably,' Paris said, dropping to her knees and crawling behind the moving legs. She thought for a second, then prodded one of them. It pinged off into the water.

The tank wobbled on one leg.

'No, no, no,' she cried as the tank toppled, rolling over and over and over before coming to a halt just short of the pier.

'Quickly, quickly,' Arabella Cod pleaded as the stilettos got louder, then stopped. 'WE'RE ALMOST THERE!'

The two of them looked to the door.

Paris's heart was beating in her eyeballs. She tried to

push the tank, but it was too heavy.

She could hear Susan Silkensocks laughing. 'NOT TALKING TODAY, ARE WE, MERMAID?'

Paris threw her backpack to the floor, spilling the contents across the pier.

Arabella Cod clutched the tank and stared down at Paris. 'You can do it, Gadget Queen.'

Paris ran at the tank, shifting it forward, and forward again. Sweat dribbled down her face. Arabella Cod pressed her hands against the glass as if she too were pushing.

The tank was almost at the edge of the pier.

'WELL, ANSWER ME, MERMAID!' Susan Silkensocks shouted.

Arabella Cod eyed the door. 'Any second and she'll realise I'm gone …'

'I can do this,' Paris said. She took a deep breath then flew at the tank one last time and –

SPLOSH!

Paris breathed a sigh of relief and peered over the edge. Two concerned-looking dolphins in shell armour were swimming fast around the mermaid, nudging her tail.

Paris scrambled to her feet and quickly collected the spilled contents of her backpack. Her hands were shaking. The last thing she needed was her mother finding evidence that it had been her who'd freed the mermaid queen.

Arabella Cod surfaced in the water, her glorious white hair gleaming in the moonlight. She pointed at the dolphins. 'My guards,' she said proudly.

Paris reached out and stroked their noses.

'WHERE. IS. MY. MERMAAAAAAAID!' came a roar from inside the factory.

'I must reward you,' Arabella Cod said, taking off one of her many necklaces and placing it in Paris's claw hand.

Paris shone her torch on it. It was a long cylinder crystal on a chain, but in the crystal she could see a tiny mermaid swimming, and a crocodile! Then a teeny tiny jellyfish swam up and down the crystal, then a shark! A little lobster floated past, then a fat fish and a dolphin! They looked real, but they were barely the size of her littlest fingernail.

'A small gift,' Arabella Cod said. 'My favourite necklace – it's thousands of years old.'

Arabella Cod winked.

And then she was gone.

The door to the factory flew open.

'Oh no,' Paris said, stuffing the necklace in her pocket and scuttling into the shadows. She pasted herself against the side of the factory and squeezed her eyes shut.

Susan Silkensocks strode out on to the pier and spotted the tank bobbing in the water.

'NOOOOOOOOOOO!' she howled.

Paris hugged her backpack tightly as the pier shook.

'That mermaid knows my plan! She'll tell them all. IT'S ALL RUIIIINNNED!'

Paris smirked; she felt quite proud. Susan Silkensocks turned and stormed back towards the factory, but then she stopped.

Paris shifted a little further into the shadows and held her breath. She was so close she could practically hear her mother's furious thoughts.

'Well, what do we have here?' she said.

Paris froze. She was a dead gadget queen.

Susan Silkensocks took a step towards Paris. Paris took a deep breath, ready to emerge from the shadows and admit what she'd done. What's the worst she could do? Turn her into a sock?

But her mother bent down to pick something up.

Paris felt a wave of relief, but it didn't last long.

'A map?' Susan Silkensocks said, turning it around and holding it up to the moonlight.

'No,' Paris whimpered.

'Ha! That silly mermaid must've left it!' she said, pausing when she saw what was written on it. 'THE CROCODILE KINGDOM?!' she roared. 'IT'S BEEN MY DREAM TO FIND THAT PLACE! Oh this is so much better than the Hidden Lagoon! I'll go there – and they'll never see me coming.' She held up her weird shell box with the F on it and kissed it. 'Arabella Cod thought she'd ruined my plan, but she's just made it *better*.'

Paris closed her eyes. 'Gadget Queen,' she whispered to herself. 'This is a *socktastrophe*.'

7

Gronnyupple the Water Witch

The strange mermaid floated in front of Beattie, Mimi and Zelda, shoving seahorse-shaped sweets into her mouth.

'Seahorse Surprise?' she mumbled through a mouthful, holding the sachet under Zelda's nose.

Zelda slowly took a sweet and popped it in her mouth, not taking her eyes off the strange mermaid.

'The name's Gronnyupple,' the mermaid said, leaning forward to bow and spilling Seahorse Surprise sweets everywhere. She began swatting about her head in an attempt to grab them.

Steve was scooped up into Gronnyupple's fist before he could say anything but Beattie was too intrigued by the mermaid to notice. She was almost certainly their age, and quite odd.

'Interesting name,' Zelda said with a smirk.

'It's a family name,' Gronnyupple said defensively.

'How did you get the false teeth?' Beattie asked. She stared over at the crumbling *Merry Mary* and thought of Hilma. 'You didn't find them on a ship, did you?'

'Nope,' Gronnyupple said, handing Beattie the empty sachet.

> FINDING FLOOP – like gloop, but it finds things. Guaranteed to transport small items short distances.

Beattie looked from the sachet to the mermaid and back again. 'Floop?' she said in disbelief.

'So you made the false teeth appear with some weird gloop?' Zelda asked, sounding unconvinced.

'Yes, a simple sachet spell I bought from the catalogue. Do you use the catalogue for magic?' Gronnyupple asked, turning to Beattie.

'Pardon?' Beattie said. 'Magic?'

 53

'Well, you're a water witch, I'd know that smell anywhere, so you must use the catalogue,' she said, swimming closer to Beattie's hair and sniffing.

Beattie began to edge away.

'Water-witch hair smells like burned Icetipple, but with overtones of power and just a hint of seaweed.'

'All right,' Zelda said, ushering the other two away from Gronnyupple. 'Time for us to go.'

'No, don't panic!' Gronnyupple said, leaning in closer. 'I'm one of you.'

'And what are we?' Zelda asked.

'Water witches,' Gronnyupple said, shoving some Seahorse Surprise back in the packet and scrunching it closed with her fist. No one noticed that Steve was inside, headbutting the packet to get out.

'I think we'd know if we were water witches,' Zelda said.

'You don't have to worry about telling me.' Gronnyupple lowered her voice to a whisper. 'I'm. One. Too.'

Zelda scrunched up her face. 'It's weird that we're speaking the same language and yet I HAVE NO IDEA WHAT YOU'RE TALKING ABOUT.'

'We're just trying to get home,' Beattie said.

'But we don't know how,' Mimi added.

'How did you get here?' Gronnyupple asked, chewing loudly and burping.

'Sunken ship,' Beattie replied.

'So sail it back.'

'We didn't exactly sail it. It sort of sailed us,' Beattie explained. 'I think it might've been its final voyage.'

'Where are you trying to get home to?' Gronnyupple asked.

'The Hidden Lagoon,' Mimi said as Zelda elbowed her in the ribs. She didn't think it was wise to admit they were from somewhere the Crocodile Kingdom mermaids didn't know about. Or perhaps they did know about the Hidden Lagoon. And perhaps they hated it.

'Ow!' Mimi cried. 'Why did you do that?'

 55

'To get you to be quiet,' Zelda whispered out of the corner of her mouth. 'For all we know, they might be hostile to mermaids from foreign seas.'

'But my ribs have nothing to do with me being quiet,' Mimi said.

Gronnyupple nodded. 'Ah, I get it, that's why you don't think you're magic. You're from one of the weird places that doesn't get the catalogue.'

'Again with the catalogue!' Zelda said.

'You should come with me,' Gronnyupple said, grabbing Beattie by the arm and trying to guide her away, but Beattie resisted.

'I can help!' Gronnyupple said cheerfully. She looked at Mimi. 'She's strange, isn't she?'

Mimi appeared to be having a conversation with a small fish.

'Where do you want to take us?' Zelda said.

'To a secret place, where snaps meet,' Gronnyupple replied, looking around to check no one was listening in. 'I'm a snap – it's what water witches in the Crocodile Kingdom are often called – snaps, water witches, magic

56

monsters, there are lots of names for us. From there I can help you get home really easily. Come on, water witches stick together, and you're going to need all the help you can get.'

'Why?' Beattie asked.

'Haven't you ever watched any mermaid films about water witches?' Gronnyupple asked.

'Nope,' Beattie said.

'Rule number one is that a water witch must always hide their powers.'

'But I don't have powers,' Beattie insisted.

Gronnyupple shoved a mouthful of Seahorse Surprise in her mouth and scrunched the bag closed again, sending Steve tumbling to the bottom. 'In *A Mermaid Called Moira*, Moira has to rely on her best friend Wayne the seal to distract everyone while her face glows because of a spell she accidentally ate, when what she was supposed to do was sit on it.'

Zelda and Beattie exchanged unconvinced looks.

'Oh, and in *Powerful Penny*,' she went on, 'which is my personal favourite film, the bully at Penny's school

57

reveals she's a water witch – and she doesn't even get to go to the school dance because music makes her transform into a whale.'

'We haven't seen either of those films,' Zelda said flatly.

'But they sound magnificent!' Mimi added.

Beattie looked at the twins and widened her eyes.

They huddled together.

'What should we do?' Beattie asked.

'It's not like we have options,' Zelda whispered. 'And apart from all the nonsense talk about a catalogue, and thinking she's magic, she seems quite nice. Weird, but harmless. What have we got to lose? She did say she could get us home *easily*.'

'Maybe she'll let us watch some of those films,' Mimi said.

'Well, we could do with a friend who knows the place. But if we're going to go with her, we need to get Hilma,' Beattie said.

'Do we have to?' Zelda groaned. 'She's happy on the *Merry Mary*, and she's pretty much evil – she'll be fine.'

Mimi shook her head. 'No, Hilma is afraid of tiny things like toes. She's like a teddy bear, really.'

'An evil, evil teddy bear,' Zelda said. 'Please can we leave the evil, evil teddy bear on the ship?'

'It's not nice to call someone an evil teddy bear, Zelda,' Beattie said.

Zelda shrugged. 'Technically, Mimi called her a teddy bear – I just added "evil, evil".'

Beattie rolled her eyes and turned to face Gronnyupple. 'We'll come with you,' she said, looking guiltily towards the *Merry Mary*. 'Just the three of us.'

'Great,' Gronnyupple said, picking up a bunch of packages with one hand and a Jellywich with the other. She shoved the Jellywich in her mouth. Beattie sneaked a glance at the labels on the parcels.

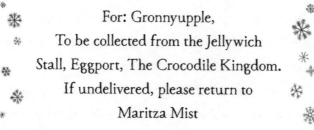

For: Gronnyupple,
To be collected from the Jellywich
Stall, Eggport, The Crocodile Kingdom.
If undelivered, please return to
Maritza Mist

'Who do you think Maritza Mist is?' Beattie whispered to Zelda as they swam through the crowds.

'Who knows,' Zelda said with a shrug. 'But I have a feeling we're going to find out.'

8

Hilma, Five Minutes Earlier

FIVE MINUTES EARLIER …

Hilma waited for the false teeth to float past her before nervously making her way to the porthole to take a peep.

She couldn't see the others anywhere. But she could see a lot of excellent hats.

'Maybe this place isn't so bad,' she mumbled, before shooting through the porthole to get a better look.

'Hello there,' came a voice. Five tiny mermaids, in five horrible brown caps, floated in front of her.

'Oh,' Hilma said, relaxing a little. 'It's not so scary out here. You're just kids.'

'Did you see a mercat swim past?' one of them asked. 'We've lost one.'

One of the others thrust a little seaweed basket under Hilma's nose.

'Is that a clump of mercats?' she said, lifting up a tiny one with a glittering yellow tail and a deafening purr. 'I thought they were a myth.'

'Can you help us find our missing mercat? We're visiting from Beluga Town and we can't go back on our sunken ship without it. Usually we have one each, but now Conrad doesn't have one.'

Conrad's lower lip began to tremble.

Hilma rolled her eyes. 'Why should I care?' she said coldly.

'We'll pay you!' one of them shouted, waving a fat bag of sharpits.

'How old are you?' Hilma said, swimming closer to inspect the bag.

'We are all five years old,' the one with the basket said proudly. 'I think ... I'm not very good at counting.'

Hilma stared at the bag of sharpits. Her stomach grumbled. She looked from the little mermaids, to the sharpits, to the stalls of delicious food. The last thing she wanted to do was hang out with tiny kids in horrible

 62

hats, but she was very hungry. And they had *a lot* of money.

'Fine,' she said, taking the horrible brown cap off Conrad's head. 'Let's find this mercat of yours. We'll retrace your swims. Where were you last?'

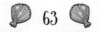

MARITZA MIST'S
WATER WITCH CATALOGUE

IMMORTALITY PASTE – SOLD OUT

A special formula brewed in the cold cauldrons of Frostopia, this rare tail paste will make you immortal. Perfect for those who want to live forever. Only two tiny tubes of these special pastes have been produced.

INSTRUCTIONS: Spread the paste evenly over your entire tail. This should stop the ageing process – whatever age you are when you put the paste on your tail will be the age you remain forever.

WARNING: This magic falls under the Water Witch Council's MEGA MAGIC category and water witches must be eighteen years and over to use this paste.

9

Paris Sets Sail

Paris didn't waste a single sockond. As soon as her mother was out of view she raced off to her ice-cream stall. If Susan Silkensocks was going to invade the Crocodile Kingdom, it was all her fault and she needed to warn them.

'Why didn't you notice you'd dropped the map?' Paris cursed herself as she hit the secret button on the ice-cream cone and slid down to her den.

The crab was in there, sitting on the table. He snapped his pincers, as if to say, *Don't do it.*

'I need to go to this spot right here,' she said, pointing at the screen where the Beattie, Mimi and Zelda dots were floating. 'Before my mother arrives and digs it all up for Mermaid World.'

The crab snapped his pincers again and looked as

concerned as a crab can look.

'Maybe it's not the Crocodile Kingdom and I've made a mistake, but my mermaids are swimming at that very spot, and who knows what will happen if my fishnapping mother gets to them first. I must warn them!'

The crab lowered his pincers.

Paris sat on her chair and adjusted her shell headphones. With a shaky hand she punched a giant shell button on the control panel and then tucked her knees up under her chin and waited.

'This might not work,' she said to the crab, who seemed to be trying, with some difficulty, to retreat into his shell.

There was a strange squeaking noise, followed by a bit of a rumble, and then with a single efficient *crunch* the whole den dropped, pulling the ice-cream stall through the pier and into the water.

Paris grabbed the control stick and steered it out to sea.

The little crab clung on to the control panel for dear life.

66

'I DID IT!' Paris roared. She leaned back in her chair. 'Gadget Queen did it!'

From land, all that could be seen was a little ice-cream hut sailing fast out to sea.

'We'll be there in sockonds!' she said with a smile as the crab covered his eyes.

THE SQUEAKER

The Crocodile Kingdom's favourite daily read

CHOPS & SLINKY ARE BACK!

The Crocodile Kingdom's cult cartoon is back, with a new series that's set to charm more mermaids than ever before! For those who have been hiding under a rock, *Chops & Slinky* are an unforgettable crocodile and eel detective duo. The *Squeaker* loves Chops the crocodile because she wears fuchsia lipstick and is fabulous, and her assistant Slinky sports a gold-fringed waistcoat!

We floated on over for a chat with Ruby Pinch, the creator of *Chops & Slinky*, at her magnificent home in Saltmont.

The *Squeaker*: Ruby Pinch, what can we expect from this new series of *Chops & Slinky*?

Ruby Pinch: A lot of Chops and a lot of Slinky! In this series they face probably their most formidable nemesis – a sunken chicken called Sylvester.

The *Squeaker*: How did you come up with the idea for *Chops & Slinky*?

Ruby Pinch: I used to live near Eggport and there was always a crocodile that swam around with an eel. One day, I left a bag of shopping outside, then the next thing I knew the crocodile was wearing my new lipstick! And the eel had taken my new gold waistcoat! I rolled back on my tail and thought, now that right there would make an excellent cartoon.

***

CHOMPTASTIC LIFESTYLE:
Our guide on how to lead your best mermaid life.

1. **NEW HOLIDAY DESTINATIONS** – Pinkly Lagoon is the new holiday hot spot you don't want to miss. Situated

in Upper Realm 9, or what humans call the Mediterranean Sea, Pinkly Lagoon has recently revamped Lazy Bay with human-style lilos that allow you to laze above the waves while keeping out of human sight. Plus, it's only a tail flick from the lagoon's infamous Vampire Rocks, where you'll find the legendary Leech Spa.

WARNING: Small numbers of human boats have been spotted in the area. Mermaids are advised to take precautions and consider practising looking like a dolphin.

WHAT TO READ: F. Ishy's latest book is bound in the finest seaweed and tells the story of Wanda Wetley, a teenage mermaid prone to disasters. An uplifting tale of momentous mermaid mishaps, it boasts a positive message about embracing imperfection, never giving up, and knowing that we are all flawed and fintastic.

10

The Chomp

At the end of Eggport's long stretch of dock there was a rock wall with a large cavernous entrance. *THE CHOMP* was scrawled on a rusty sign hanging above it.

The four of them (and Steve in the Seahorse Surprise bag) floated on the spot, watching as mermaid after mermaid filed into the cave.

'HURRY UP,' a mermaid shouted over them to her friends behind. 'THE NIBBLEHOLLOW TRAIN LEAVES IN TWO MINUTES!'

'The Chomp is a train?' Beattie asked.

Gronnyupple grinned. 'It's a whole underground network of trains, run by a bunch of crocodiles.'

'Humans have something similar,' Beattie said. 'Only without the crocodiles.'

Gronnyupple spat out some Seahorse Surprise. 'Don't say the H-word.'

'You mean "human"?' Zelda said.

Gronnyupple covered her ears as they followed the crowds inside. 'Lalalalalalala horrible word lalalalalala!'

'Jiggling jellyfish on sticks,' Mimi whispered.

Beattie and Zelda stopped dead in their tracks when they saw the place.

Past the uninviting entrance was a grand hall crammed full of mermaids, sipping cups of takeaway foam shakes, reading seaweed papers and dashing for trains. A couple of mermaids floated next to them, complaining about there being too many tourists in a place called Emerald Cove.

'This is INCREDIBLE!' Zelda shouted, her voice echoing off the glistening green walls.

At the far end of the vast cave, a line of crocodiles lay side by side in a long row. Every so often a green light would flash above one of them, their mouth would open and inside would be a sign, saying things like:

**NORTHBOUND TO NIBBLEHOLLOW,
LEAVING NOW. PLATFORM 11.**

**SOUTHBOUND TO JELLYHOOD,
LEAVING NOW, PLATFORM 4.**

'Which platform do we need?' Beattie asked.

'And how do we buy a token to get on the train?'
Mimi said.

Beattie spun round. 'Token?'

73

Mimi nodded and pointed at a poster.

NO TOKEN, NO CHOMP.
Two sharpits per token.

'Sharpits?!' Beattie cried. 'I don't even know what that is.'

'It's money,' Gronnyupple said, opening her hand to reveal a couple of little metal bits shaped like triangles. 'You put two in that treasure chest over there, and then you get a token to ride. But I don't have enough for everyone. Are you sure you don't have any?'

Beattie shook her head.

'I have an idea,' Mimi said, swimming off towards the treasure chest. Gronnyupple followed her.

'Wait,' Zelda said. 'Mimi, how did you buy that Jellywich you were eating earlier?'

Beattie watched as Mimi casually swam over to a group of mermaids chatting by the treasure chest. They all had takeaway foam shakes in their hands.

'Oh no,' Zelda said slowly. 'I know what she's going to do.'

'How?' Beattie asked.

'We're *twins*,' Zelda said. 'Plus I can see her flexing her little finger. She's going to fin-fu something.'

Quicker than Beattie could say 'oh cod', the takeaway foam shakes were knocked from the hands of the mermaids by something incredibly fast and Mimi-shaped. The foam frothed out, creating a cloud around the treasure chest.

'WHO DID THAT?' one of the mermaids roared.

'MY HAIR IS SOAKED!' another screamed. 'IN FOAM!'

As the cloud began to clear, Beattie caught a flash of Mimi grabbing a handful of coins from the treasure chest. 'Three tokens please,' she said, dropping the sharpits into the treasure chest. The pufferfish in charge spat the tokens at her and she swam back over.

'I left my fin-fu necklace in the treasure chest,' she said, placing a token in their hands. 'To make up for the sharpits I took.'

'But that's your favourite necklace!' Zelda cried.

'Otherwise it would be stealing,' Mimi said.

A crocodile opened its mouth to reveal *SALTMONT, PLATFORM 5*.

'THAT'S US!' Gronnyupple shouted, licking some foam shake off her hair.

The tunnel to platform five was dark, with faulty green lights that flickered as the mermaids swam past. Crowds swarmed the tunnels, all racing to get to the Chomp train.

Posters lined the walls.

Don't miss *The Five Flops of Wanda Wetley*, the latest bestselling novel by F. Ishy.

'SHOCKEY!' Zelda exclaimed when she saw the next poster. Shockey was Zelda's favourite sport in the Hidden Lagoon.

'I can't believe they have it in the Crocodile Kingdom too!'

The poster showed two teams, the Jellyhood Jocks and the Saltmont Slammers battling it out. The Jellyhood Jocks were riding side-saddle on a cluster of jellyfish and the Saltmont Slammers rode crocodiles with gold-painted claws and jaws.

'We'd definitely beat the Lobstertown Loons if we were allowed to ride on *crocodiles*. Maybe I'll bring one back.'

'Come on, Zelda,' Beattie said, pulling her further down the tunnel.

The platform was crammed to bursting with mermaids waiting patiently. There was no sign of the train, and a mermaid next to them was reading a seaweed magazine.

'Their magazine is called the *Squeaker*,' Beattie whispered, trying to catch a glimpse of what was in it.

There was a rumble. A series of snapping sounds. And before they could blink the Chomp lurched into view.

The whole thing was covered in gorgeous green shells, and as Beattie got closer to the edge of the platform she saw that each carriage was sitting on top of a crocodile.

'Wow,' Beattie mouthed as a mermaid shoved her

head first into the carriage, where her nose got wedged in another mermaid's armpit.

'Oh wow,' Zelda said as she squashed in next to Beattie. 'It's more incredible than toast!'

'Tourists,' Gronnyupple said with a nervous laugh to the mermaid next to her. 'It's like they've never ridden a Chomp before.'

The shell-covered doors closed and the Chomp began to move. Beattie peered out of the large oyster shell-shaped windows and could just make out the crocodile legs moving beneath them.

'This is so *cool*,' Zelda whispered, nodding at an elderly mermaid who was swimming slowly above their heads, guided by an equally elderly-looking sea cucumber.

The long bench-like seats on either side of the carriage were completely full, so Beattie, Zelda and Mimi held on to plaited seaweed ropes, swinging back and forth as the carriage clattered on through the dark rock tunnel.

The posters lining the walls of the carriage were all alike – mermaids posing with pufferfish, wearing different colours of lipstick and eyeshadow. Each poster had the word 'FLUBIÉRE' on it.

'What's Flubiére?' Beattie asked, just as a mermaid in a Flubiére T-shirt appeared, accompanied by some lipstick-wearing pufferfish.

An intercom crackled.

'Welcome aboard the Chomp. Make-up brand Flubiére will be advertising its new colour palettes in selected carriages today. Please don't be alarmed by the promotional pufferfish. Thank you.'

One of the pufferfish began combing a teenage mermaid's eyebrows with its tail. Another floated in front of Gronnyupple's face, its lips glowing bright purple. She stared at it for a moment then tapped the lips, changing them to coral pink. She tapped again, changing them to a dark plum colour.

Beattie couldn't believe her eyes.

'Did you see that?' she whispered to the twins.

Gronnyupple nodded at the dark plum colour and the fish lunged at her. Beattie thought the fish was going to eat her nose, but instead it kissed her lips, transferring the deep plum colour on to hers. She inspected herself in a mirror and nodded. The mermaid wearing the Flubiére T-shirt approached carrying a bubble, and inside was a little shell filled with the plum lip gloss. Gronnyupple handed over two sharpits, burst the bubble and stuffed the lip gloss in her bag.

Although most of the mermaids in the carriage had crocodile-patterned tails, one – with a scaled tail like Beattie, Mimi and Zelda – was sitting on a bench, his

eyes glued to a flipped-open shell. Inside, it looked like two tiny fish were weaving through a coral maze.

'It looks like a game,' Zelda said, noticing what Beattie was looking at.

'It's called Flippit,' Gronnyupple said. 'I tried to play it once but my fish wouldn't move.'

'Were they dead?' Zelda asked.

'I don't know,' Gronnyupple said. 'I didn't ask them.'

A stingray rose from the floor of the carriage and pointed its tail at Beattie.

'AAAARGH!' Beattie screamed. Steve also screamed from inside the Seahorse Surprise bag, but it was muffled so nobody noticed him.

Mimi casually held out her Chomp token. The stingray zapped it.

'It's checking the tokens,' Mimi said. 'I read about it on the Chomp poster.'

'This is *bewildering*,' Zelda said. 'I'm like a cat on an ice cream in this place!'

'That doesn't make any sense,' Beattie said. She looked up and saw a map of the Chomp route. The train line forked, splitting into two long lines that reminded her of open crocodile jaws. 'Eggport, Nibblehollow, Lava,' Beattie whispered, reading all the stops. 'Jellyhood, Emerald Cove.' She stopped at the one right before the line forked. 'Saltmont city.' A green light came on next to it.

'We will shortly be arriving in Saltmont. Saltmont next stop,' the intercom boomed.

'Time to go, Doris,' the old mermaid wheezed at her sea cucumber. It was getting a makeover from one of the pufferfish. 'You look very pretty.'

The Chomp ground to a halt and the sea cucumber floated slowly past them and out of the door.

'We've reached our destination!' Gronnyupple shouted. She turned to Beattie and whispered, 'No magic until we're safely hidden in the secret meeting place.' She winked.

'I don't even know how to do magic,' Beattie groaned.

Saltmont Chomp station was ten times the size of Eggport, and the mermaids that swam around it were a lot trendier, with long waistcoats and short crop tops, bejewelled clutch bags and shell backpacks, perfectly straight hair and fishtail pleats. A lot of them had crocodile-print tails, but there was a great variety of others too – rainbow tails and bright red ones, the occasional eel-shaped one and even a translucent one.

Beattie smiled. 'Saltmont must be one of the biggest mermaid cities in the world!'

There was a deafening crunching sound behind them.

'DIVE!' Gronnyupple screamed, pushing them aside just as a wayward Chomp train came crashing through the wall and skidded to a halt in the middle of the station.

Beattie steadied herself and dusted down her tail. 'Is it meant to do that?!'

Gronnyupple frowned. 'No. It's never done that before.'

Mermaids floated around it in silent shock.

'Something strange is going on,' Gronnyupple said. 'This isn't the first unusual thing that's happened.'

Beattie watched as a tiny crab scuttled across the floor and out of the station.

'Where's your secret meeting place?' Zelda said, helping them all outside.

Gronnyupple grinned at the mention of it. 'It's a two-minute swim. Or a five-hour one if I get lost again.'

FUNNY LUMPY COMES TO THE CROCODILE KINGDOM (for five nights only)

Wendelle Water from Beluga Town is currently in the Kingdom staging her latest play, which has been touring around other mermaid regions – including our friends in Octopolli and Pinkly Lagoon.

It's set in a Shrimpol station, and for any of you who haven't visited Beluga Town, a Shrimpol station is a lot like a kelp fuel or human petrol station.

When a beluga whale called Lumpy begins work at the local Shrimpol station he thinks he's just going to be filling up the other whales with Shrimpol so they can pull sleighs. Then he realises he can speak to the mermaids riding the sleighs, and that he is quite the comedian!

'It's basically a comedy show about a beluga whale who works at a Shrimpol station,' Wendelle Water explained.

Beluga Town's very own Shrimpol station owner, and friendliest face, Moira Wet, inspired the play.

'Oh, I'm sure it's not inspired by me. I just fill up the Shrimpol tanks and do my bit for Beluga Town!' Moira Wet said chirpily.

When asked what she thought was Lumpy's funniest line, Wendelle Water smiled and simply said, 'You'll have to see it and decide for yourself.'

Funny Lumpy is showing at Saltmont's Greenlilly Theatre NOW. Don't miss it!

11

Hilma Sees a Play

Hilma floated at the back of the theatre, sipping a foam shake.

The seaweed curtain rose and a mermaid dressed in a fake beluga whale costume flopped on to the stage and began singing about being both funny and lumpy.

'We have lots of beluga whales in Beluga Town,' Conrad the tiny mermaid said as he began to count them all on his fingers, 'one, two, three, four, three.'

'I don't see any mercats in here,' Hilma said, floating towards the stage. 'EXCUSE ME, OI! FUNNY LUMPY! YES, YOU! STOP SINGING. HAVE YOU SEEN A MERCAT?'

FIVE SECONDS LATER …

'Well, they'll throw you out of the theatre for anything these days, won't they!' Hilma spat, slapping letters off the sign so it now read *UNNY UMPY*. 'The mercat wasn't there, so where were you before you went to see *Funny Lumpy*?'

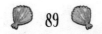

12

Paris and the Seagull

Paris sat on the edge of the ice-cream stall, staring out to sea. A fat fish popped its head out of the water.

'Before you ask,' Paris said, blowing stray hair out of her face, 'I'm on my way to warn some mermaids about my mother. It sounds weird, I know. And no, I have not brushed my teeth today. I really should've brought my toothbrush with me, but I left in a hurry and forgot it. Do fish brush their teeth? I think I might've been at sea too long.'

The fish blinked at her for a second, then launched out of the water and straight over the stall, grabbing one of the ice-cream cones as it went.

'Well, that was rude,' Paris said.

There was a swishing sound. Paris leaned nervously

over the edge and saw a hundred other fat fish faces poking out of the water.

'Uh-oh,' she said as they all leapt for the ice-cream cones.

13

Paris and the Sharks

Paris tipped the last of the multicoloured sprinkles into her mouth and dropped the tub at her feet.

'I'd better get there soon, or I'll starve,' she said to the crab.

The water was getting choppier.

'And I think a storm is brewing,' she called up to the crab as she descended to her den.

The mermaid tracker was still blinking – but Beattie, Mimi and Zelda had moved a bit further west. If they *were* in the Crocodile Kingdom, it was obviously very big.

Paris looked up slowly from the control panel. She was sure she'd seen a flash of grey tail.

'A mermaid?' she said excitedly.

The den was rocking violently from side to side now, and the water was so murky she could barely see anything. A couple of gadgets fizzed and flickered. The string of sock bunting on the Susan Cam pinged off, sending socks flying about the den. Paris tried to steady herself but fell forwards, headbutting the glass wall. And then she saw it. A huge great white shark floating in the murky water.

She shot back up to top deck and peered over the edge. The great white wasn't alone – at least twenty shark fins were circling the ice-cream hut.

'WHY DOES EVERYTHING LIKE ICE CREAM?' Paris shouted at the sky. She turned to look at the water. 'I DON'T HAVE ANY ICE CREAM LEFT, I WAS ROBBED BY FISH! NO FOOD HERE!'

She stopped, and gulped.

Maybe there was still food on the stall …

The waves rose up high and came crashing down.

'NOBODY PANIC!' Paris yelled as the crab scuttled on to her head and tried to burrow under her hair. The stall tipped sideways, taking on a lot of water. It began to sink.

Paris grabbed her backpack and held on tightly to her tiny mermaid compass.

Another, bigger wave crashed down, sending Paris flying. She clung on to the edge of the stall, her legs dangling over the side.

An alarm sounded.

'Susan Cam?' she spluttered. 'But she can't be here! Not ye–'

Another impressive wave shattered what was left of the ice-cream stall, sending Paris spiralling down into the dark, shark-infested waters below ...

14

The Out-of-Bounds Whale Bus

Paris was somersaulting and spluttering in the water, expecting a great white to take a bite out of her at any sockond. She was struggling to breathe.

A shark came up behind her and grabbed her plait in its teeth.

Paris squeezed her eyes shut.

It shook her – just once – and then let her go.

She winced and waited, but nothing happened.

She dared a peek. The sharks were still there, circling her, but she felt strange. Her legs felt longer and more floppy. She sighed with relief, and then realised she shouldn't be able to do that underwater.

Her little mermaid compass floated down past her. The light next to the word 'MERMAID' was flashing. 'But – wait, WHAT? WHOA,' Paris said as she looked down. 'MY LEGS!' she cried, as clearly as if she was speaking out of water. 'THEY'VE GONE!'

In their place was a beautiful, pearly-coloured tail!

The smallest shark in the group swam up and pushed its nose towards her necklace.

'Is that what transformed me?' Paris said. 'When you shook me? It must be *magic*.'

Another shark floated next to her and offered her its fin. Reluctantly, she grabbed hold – and off they shot! The other sharks followed. They were giving her a swimming lesson. She flicked her tail back and forth, and they went even faster. Her crab friend sailed past on the back of another shark.

'WOOOOOHOOOOOOOO!' Paris yelled, letting go of the shark's fin and somersaulting through the sea. 'I'M A GADGET QUEEN *AND* A WEIRD MUTANT FISH HUMAN! THIS IS THE BEST DAY OF MY LIIIIIIIIIFE!'

A dark aeroplane-shaped shadow descended and the sharks scattered.

'Wait!' Paris cried. 'Come back!'

There was a strange whirring noise that echoed so loudly she had to cover her ears.

Then came a SPLOSH! And the thing that made it came speeding towards her.

'Mother?' Paris said, blinking in disbelief. Her mouth hung open as her mother, eyes tightly closed, arms outstretched, shot past in a perfect dive pose. Her legs were concealed by a magnificent fake mermaid tail!

The Susan Cam that was sinking to the depths began beeping out of control.

Paris swam as fast as she could. She was going to beat her mother to the Crocodile Kingdom and warn them all!

A horn sounded – about an inch from her head.

'OW!' she cried, rubbing her left ear and half expecting it to have blasted right off.

A strange jellyfish with a hollow horn strapped to the top of it floated on the spot.

'YOU ARE FLOATING IN DANGEROUS HUMAN TERRITORY,' came a voice from the horn.

Paris poked her eye right in it to get a look. 'Who's saying that?'

'QUENTIN WILL ENSURE YOU BOARD THE WHALE BUS TO SAFETY. WHAT IS YOUR NAME AND HOME REGION?'

Paris looked down at her tail. They thought she was a mermaid!

A huge whale emerged from the depths and pulled up next to her, with a rickety old green human bus strapped to it.

Behind the wheel was an ancient-looking mermaid with only one tiny tuft of hair. She pulled a lever and the door opened.

'I'm Jelly,' she said. 'We chatted earlier on my horn, which I strapped to Quentin's head. Quentin is my jellyfish. Now, where are you from?'

'The … crocodile one,' Paris mumbled nervously. She glanced around, looking for help. She couldn't get caught, and she couldn't let her mother get ahead of her.

'Well, technically there's two crocodile ones,' Jelly

said. 'You've got the Crocodile Kingdom, but then occasionally Rainbow Landing also has crocodiles.'

'The first one – the Crocodile Kingdom,' Paris said, faltering slightly.

Jelly peered out from behind her glasses. 'You don't seem very sure?'

'Oh I am, I'm just, you know … *bad day*.'

Jelly nodded and pulled out an old human telephone. 'I'll call the Crocodile Kingdom and tell them you're here, since you look underage. Name?'

'Oh, no, it's –' Paris said, giggling nervously. 'Wait, does that phone *work* down here?'

'Like a charm,' Jelly said, punching in some numbers. A small fish popped out of the receiver. 'Crocodile Kingdom mermaid,' she said to the fish. 'Name is Ohnoits, found and to be returned to the Shelmont City stop.' The fish popped back into the receiver and Paris saw the wire bulging where the fish was swimming along fast inside it. The wire wafted in the water and came to an end not far from the whale bus. Paris watched as the fish shot out of the end of the wire and went swimming off.

 100

'You know that's not how humans use phones,' Paris said.

'It is,' Jelly said. 'Only they don't use fish. I believe they use spiders. Now, swim on board.'

Paris did her best but she was still a little unsteady manoeuvring her tail.

Human paintings were tacked to the bus walls, and a tiny shoal of fish was attempting to eat the one of a bowl of oranges.

Paris took a seat next to an old man and an old lady mermaid. They had wrinkled tails and matching *Chops & Slinky* T-shirts. The old lady mermaid was holding on tightly to a human shopping trolley.

'It's a souvenir,' she said when she spotted Paris looking at it. She tapped her nose and winked. 'We've been on land.'

'With your tails?' Paris asked.

'It's amazing how far you can get on land with a shopping trolley and an oar,' the old man mermaid said, coughing.

Quentin swam past with the horn strapped to his head. 'HIGHLY ILLEGAL BEHAVIOUR,' Jelly's voice bellowed through the horn. 'DON'T LISTEN TO THESE TWO, OHNOITS.'

The two old mermaids leaned back on the bench and grinned.

'Worth every police car chase,' the old lady mermaid said.

Paris smiled and inspected the necklace Arabella Cod had given her – she could still see things swimming around in there. A crocodile. A shark. A jellyfish. A lobster. A fat fish. A dolphin.

She gasped.

The mermaid was gone! But she'd been replaced with something else. There was a human – a tiny little Paris in her pom-pom-fringed summer dress.

'NO WAY!' Paris said, shaking the thing back and forth twice.

She felt tightness in her tail. There was a small pop and suddenly her head felt bigger, and her arms felt tiny.

'Where did the nice little mermaid go?' the old lady mermaid asked, slowly bending over to peer into her shopping trolley, as if Paris might be hiding in there.

'I'm right here!' Paris said with a laugh. But it came out as 'EEEeeeEEE A-AAK! K! EEEee.'

'I was sure there was a mermaid here,' the old man

mermaid said slowly. 'But perhaps she was always a dolphin.'

'EEeeeeeEeEeEeEe! A-kk, eee!' Paris tried again, but they weren't listening.

She held the necklace up, inspecting it like she did her gadgets. *Maybe* she thought, her heart beating fast, *the number of shakes determines which creature I transform into …*

The shark had shaken her once, so she tried giving it one shake. With a *snap*, she was a mermaid again.

'She's back!' the old lady mermaid cried.

'Twice for dolphin,' Paris said, shaking it twice. And with a flubbery bang she was a dolphin again! 'An excellent gadget,' she concluded.

Quentin floated past and came to an abrupt halt next to Paris the dolphin.

'NO STRAY DOLPHINS!' came Jelly's exasperated voice. 'REMOVE THE DOLPHIN.'

'That's our dolphin!' the old lady mermaid cried. 'I remember it … I think.'

The door to the bus swung open and another

mermaid flopped on. Paris felt a bit sick when she saw who it was.

'Crocodile Kingdom,' Susan Silkensocks snapped at Jelly, before swimming on to the bus.

Paris covered the necklace with one of her flippers – it was just the kind of curious cool thing her mum would steal from a dolphin.

Susan Silkensocks swam with her obviously fake tail and took a seat across the aisle from Paris the now-dolphin. Paris could see a clear film over her mother's face, though it was barely noticeable. Paris slumped over, her dolphin nose drooping. Her mother must've created some high-tech breathing mask, probably with the help of some clever scientist lady and a lot of money.

Paris clutched the necklace tightly. As long as she was a dolphin, her mother would never know it was her.

MARITZA MIST'S
WATER WITCH CATALOGUE

WARDROBE WHIZZ

A fun little number for you fashionistas out there. With the Wardrobe Whizz, you can change your outfit with the click of a finger.

INSTRUCTIONS: Rest the shell on the tip of your tail and click your finger. Comes with three hundred couture outfits, ten fancy-dress costumes and a selection of hats.

15

Twinkors

'And *here* –' Gronnyupple said grandly, pausing for effect – 'it is.'

'Twinkors,' Beattie said, blinking at the place.

'This is where I have secret snap meetings,' Gronnyupple said.

'It's a launderette,' Zelda said flatly. 'Called Twinkors.'

Beattie, Mimi and Zelda stared at it.

'Well, at least we got to ride on the Chomp,' Zelda said, turning to leave.

'Wait!' Gronnyupple pleaded, swimming up to the Twinkors sign. 'Erm, look at how … beautiful it … is.'

The sign had been half eaten by small fish and the two large triangular windows had been claimed by a family of suckerfish, so you couldn't even see if anything was going on inside.

The 'S' on the sign made a groaning sound and fell off, hitting the seabed with a clang.

'Are you both thinking what I'm thinking?' Beattie whispered.

'Yes, it's beautiful!' Mimi said.

Beattie and Zelda stared at her.

'Well,' Beattie finally said, 'we're already here, so we might as well give Gronnyupple five minutes.'

'Five minutes,' Zelda said. 'That's it. Then we find our *own* way home. I don't believe anything she says. And I don't believe she's going to help us.'

Inside, Beattie floated awkwardly near the door. Twinkors was deserted – and it looked like it had been for years. Fabulous unwanted mermaid clothes floated about the room, along with a crocodile. She was a hardy-looking reptile with extra-long eyelashes. A bottle of Kelpskey hung from the corner of her mouth. When she opened her jaw, Beattie could see that her teeth had been painted with colourful patterns.

Beattie, Mimi and Zelda pasted themselves against the wall as she floated past.

'Oh, Lady Rusty won't hurt you!' Gronnyupple said with a hearty laugh.

'The crocodile is called Lady Rusty?' Zelda asked, trying to stifle a snort. 'Is she your pet?'

Gronnyupple was now the one to snort. 'No! She *owns* this place.'

'Really?' Beattie said in disbelief.

'Oh yes,' Gronnyupple said. 'She's the original snap. But now she just kind of floats around like an uncontrollable decoration.'

Lady Rusty swam straight into the wall.

There was a high-pitched scream.

'Steve!' Beattie cried, feeling about in her hair for him before seeing Gronnyupple was holding him firmly in her hand.

'Calm down, seahorse thing!' she said. 'I thought you were a Seahorse Surprise.'

Steve stopped screaming. 'What is a Seahorse Surprise?!'

'It's a sweet, shaped like a seahorse – you eat the first succulent jelly layer and there's another surprise sweet inside.'

'YOU WERE TRYING TO PULL MY HEAD OFF!' Steve shouted.

Gronnyupple widened her eyes in frustration. 'Yes, because I thought you were a Seahorse Surprise. You were in my sweet packet.'

'I thought you were in the false teeth, Steve,' Beattie said, placing him gently back inside them.

'No, that monster grabbed me and stuffed me in her packet of sweets. I've been shouting for help for the last hour!'

'He's –' Zelda began to explain to Gronnyupple.

'A *miracle*,' Steve said grandly.

'He's my talking seahorse,' Beattie said. 'He likes to sleep in false teeth. Must be really weird for you to see a talking seahorse.'

Gronnyupple shoved a handful of Seahorse Surprises in her mouth and swallowed them in one gulp. 'Not really. I've been to Flicko City in Pinkly Lagoon, so I've seen thousands of talking seahorses. I went on holiday there once – we stopped on our way to Vampire Rocks. Is that where you got it? Flicko City?'

Beattie looked down at Steve nestled in the false teeth.

'*Thousands?*' Steve mouthed sadly.

'Looks like *someone* isn't a miracle after all,' Zelda teased.

 111

Steve stuck his nose in the air. 'Still more of a miracle than you, normal half-fish person!'

'Where are the other water witches?' Mimi chirped.

'It's just me,' Gronnyupple said.

'You're the only one?' Zelda said.

'The only one,' Gronnyupple said, turning to smile at Beattie. 'Until *you*.'

'And this is … er, your secret meeting place?' Beattie asked, swimming around. 'Where you meet with … you.'

Gronnyupple nodded. 'An old couple used to work here, but then they went travelling on land, wearing T-shirts that say things like *"I GOT LEGS AND ALL I GOT WAS THIS LOUSY T-SHIRT"*. The launderette crumbled and got old and so I thought it would be perfect for secret water witch things. No one swims in here any more. It's like a vintage clothes shop, really – there's lots of great stuff floating around. Take anything you want.'

Beattie grabbed a studded belt that was floating past her and tried it on.

'Silly question,' Zelda said, 'but how do you plan to help us get home?'

'Through a friend,' Gronnyupple said. She swam over to a big box of BUBBLE JIM'S washing powder and pulled out a seaweed map.

Beattie's eyes widened when she saw it. It was a map of the world, with all the human bits too. There were various sparkly dots showing place names Beattie recognised from her mum's stories. All these mermaid territories no one believed existed.

'Where's your Hidden Lagoon?' Gronnyupple asked.

Beattie pointed to the spot in the Pacific. There was nothing on the map – no name, no sparkly dot.

'Ah, unknown territory,' Gronnyupple said. 'Interesting.' She scrawled 'The Hidden Lagoon' on the map.

She looked up and stared at Beattie. 'Have you ever been to any other mermaid kingdom, aside from your Hidden Lagoon?'

'No,' Beattie said. 'We didn't know any definitely existed until we came here! Most mermaids in our lagoon think the Crocodile Kingdom is a myth.'

'The Hidden Lagoon must be an area that doesn't get the catalogue any more,' Gronnyupple said, letting the map float off and hit Lady Rusty in the face. 'That means, anyone who is a water witch would never know – there would be no magic to use.'

'She keeps going on about a *catalogue*,' Zelda whispered to Mimi, but Mimi was too busy helping Lady Rusty peel the map off her face.

'Magic used to be much more common, but then ages ago a terrible human got hold of some magic near a place called Amberberg and nearly destroyed us. After that, mermaids were spooked and cracked down on magic for fear of it falling into the wrong hands – or worse, *human* hands. As the years passed, and water witches hid their powers, mermaids stopped believing in magic.'

'But even if it's true, how did I become a water witch?' Beattie asked.

'That's the thing,' Gronnyupple whispered. 'No one knows why some mermaids are water witches.' She shoved a Seahorse Surprise in her mouth as it floated past. 'It's like a rare disease. Only it's excellent.'

'So you think we're all water witches?' Zelda said.

'No,' Gronnyupple said. 'Just Beattie.'

'How can you be sure?' Zelda scoffed.

Gronnyupple tapped her nose. 'Smelt it.'

'I don't believe all this water witch stuff anyway!' Zelda said, clenching her fists. 'And I bet you don't have a catalogue that you order magic from. It sounds made-up!'

Gronnyupple plucked an ice-blue coloured catalogue from behind where Lady Rusty was floating.

MARITZA MIST'S
WATER WITCH CATALOGUE

In her other hand Gronnyupple held up the packages she'd been carrying since they'd met in Eggport. 'And look here, I just received my latest delivery.'

'I … don't believe it,' Zelda said, flicking through the catalogue. 'This can't be real.'

There was a bang and a gigantic fat fish flopped out of the washing machine by Beattie's tail.

'Ah!' Gronnyupple said. 'Krilky wants me. Come on!'

'Krilky?' they all said at once.

'My friend!' Gronnyupple said cheerily. 'But we can't tell anyone we're friends.'

'Why not?' Beattie asked slowly.

'You'll see,' Gronnyupple said, then stuck her head into the washing machine. 'Coming!'

'If this ends with us getting eaten and turned

into Seahorse Surprise,' Zelda said through gritted teeth, 'I'm blaming you, Beatts.'

'Greased up the sides with a bit of magic, didn't I,' Gronnyupple said, slapping the washing machine proudly. 'Works extra fast now.'

Mimi stared intently at the fish

flopping about on the edge of the washing machine. 'I'm very sorry to hear you're having a bad day, sir.'

'You first,' Gronnyupple said, shoving Mimi into the washing machine.

She disappeared.

'Wait. Think about how weird this is,' Zelda said, pulling on Beattie's tail, but Beattie was sucked inside and disappeared.

'HELLO?' Zelda said, sticking her head in the washing machine. She swam backwards and crossed her arms angrily. 'You were meant to be helping us get home, for cod's sake! I'm staying here.'

'Suit yourself,' Gronnyupple said with a burp as she dived in after Beattie.

'I'm not getting inside a washing machine,' Zelda said.

'ME NEITHER,' Steve said, sticking his nose in the air defiantly.

They both turned slowly and looked at each other.

'I don't want to wait here with you,' Zelda said.

'And I don't want to wait here with *you*,' Steve replied.

They narrowed their eyes at each other, then raced towards the old washing machine and squished inside.

MARITZA MIST'S
WATER WITCH CATALOGUE

FAST FORWARD!

Wish you could get everything done faster?
Ever wanted to move so fast no one can see you?
Well, this is the spell for you – it'll speed you up!

INSTRUCTIONS: Chant the spell, while
holding the supplied jellyfish. If the jellyfish
glows, the spell has worked.

Fast as a flash!
Fat as a whale!
Speed and stealth
all in my tail!

LEGAL NOTE: This spell must not be used for robbing.

16

Paris Has a Bumpy Ride

Paris sat in the seat across the aisle from Susan Silkensocks, who was sitting with her hands in her lap, her fingers tightly wrapped around that silly shell box with the F on it. She was trying to blend in – just a normal mermaid on a whale bus, with an almost-real tail.

'Before we take off, we have a special presentation from Flubiére. Please don't be alarmed by the promotional pufferfish,' came a voice over the loudspeaker.

A bunch of pufferfish with brightly coloured lips made their way through the bus.

Paris clutched the crystal necklace. Shaking it made her morph, so all she had to do was *not shake* the necklace. As long as she remained a dolphin, she'd be disguised and Susan Silkensocks would have no idea

 120

it was her sitting right across the aisle.

All she had to do was *not shake the necklace.*

The horn on Quentin's head honked, and the pufferfish left the bus. Before Paris knew what was happening, the door slammed shut and the whale took off, the bus rattling madly on top of it.

Paris fell off her seat and morphed into a jellyfish.

'Aa-aa-aa-aa-ar-gh!' she screamed, jiggling about, but it came out as jellyfish silence. She looked over at Susan Silkensocks. It was fine – she was distracted by the view of the magnificent canyons and fish.

'THANK YOU, CANYONS AND FISH!' Paris cried, but it came out as jellyfish silence.

She tried frantically to steady the necklace with her stingers, but it was no good. She felt herself stretching and –

FLIIIIPSLIIIP!

She was transformed into a shark.

She bounced up and down, trying to hold the necklace steady in her teeth. Susan Silkensocks began humming.

122

'*Just no more changing, just no more changing,*' Paris said over and over.

There was a bang, the whale veered to the right, sending the necklace pinging out of Paris's shark teeth.

She felt herself shrink.

Susan Silkensocks began turning towards her.

Paris could feel the sweat tricking down her forehead and into her nose. She could feel toes.

'NO!' she cried, as bubbles started streaming through her nose. She looked down and saw her human legs! She floated up fast and hit the ceiling of the bus with a gentle *twang*.

'Did someone say NO?' Susan Silkensocks asked, looking around the bus suspiciously.

Paris held on to the ceiling for dear life, her eyes wide. Susan Silkensocks couldn't look up. She couldn't look up! Paris puffed out her cheeks – she couldn't breathe! She grabbed the necklace and frantically shook it, her face turning blue.

'And where did that dolphin go?' Susan Silkensocks asked the old couple, just as Paris morphed into a

 123

crocodile and landed back down on the seat with a squelch.

Susan Silkensocks screamed.

'It's our crocodile, he's not a dolphin,' the old lady mermaid said slowly.

'I thought,' the old man mermaid said, even more slowly, 'we had a dolphin.'

'Did you say diner?' the old lady mermaid said. 'I only eat at the Crunch Diner, because it sells sunken human food.'

'I know that, dear,' the old man mermaid wheezed. 'But I said *dolphin*.'

'No one eats dolphin,' the old lady mermaid said.

Paris leaned her huge crocodile head against the window and sighed.

The whale bus slowed as they approached a large rock wall covered in coral. Strange green eyes on a stone crocodile began flashing as the coral fell away.

Susan Silkensocks wriggled in her seat. 'In we go!'

The whale bus floated smoothly into the tunnel and began rising upwards. Unlike the boats, which were directed to dock in Eggport, the bus went straight to Saltmont.

'Wow, look at it,' Paris said, though it came out as 'GNASH, GNASH, GNASH.'

'I hear chomping!' the old lady mermaid cheered.

The whale weaved in and out of huge see-through tubes filled with mermaids swimming up and down.

Below them, Paris could see castle-shaped buildings with spiked turrets and jagged stone bridges connecting them. Clam cars whizzed past on either side, diving to avoid crocodiles. Tiny flashing jellyfish marked out the routes the clam cars could take. Every so often they were stopped by a cluster of crabs forming a cross to signify *STOP*.

Huge billboards, like the ones in Lobstertown, displayed moving pictures of a cartoon crocodile and a cartoon eel.

'Wow,' Paris said, which came out as 'GNASH' again. She turned to her mother and practically slipped off her seat.

125

Susan Silkensocks was sneakily squeezing out of the window!

Paris thrashed about, trying to get out of her seat, but her crocodile body felt heavy and slow. She charged as fast as she could at the open window and tried to squeeze through.

There was a long squeaking sound as her crocodile head slid slowly through the gap before finally jamming.

'Is my trolley talking?' the old lady mermaid asked. She put an ear to it. 'I think it is.'

Paris frantically tried to wriggle free. When she realised she couldn't, she tried to grab the necklace with her teeth. If she could morph into something smaller she'd be free!

She gnashed and gnashed and grabbed it right between two teeth. But when she tried to shake it she realised the necklace was stuck. She couldn't move it enough to shake it.

She sighed as mermaids stopped and pointed at the whale bus with a crocodile head jammed in the window.

The bus came to a stop at a sign that said *Downtown Saltmont*.

'EVERY FIN OFF!' Jelly shouted, and the old couple moved slowly along the bus, smacking their trolley into every seat on the way.

A mermaid in an official-looking hat with a triangle on top swam up to Paris the crocodile.

'Unofficial crocodile?' he said.

Jelly threw her hands in the air. 'I didn't spot it!'

'It'll need to be approved by Her Fishiness.' He tapped Paris's crocodile nose. 'You'll need official permission from Dragonholm Palace to swim here. I'll escort you there myself.'

Paris looked around desperately as Jelly appeared with a huge razorfish to saw through the window frame.

Thousands of mermaids swam past. Not one of them was Susan Silkensocks.

Paris had lost her!

Jelly finally sawed through the window frame and Paris swam free. She shook her head madly to morph into something else, but with the necklace still stuck in her teeth it wasn't enough to make it work!

'I'M A GIRL, NOT A CROCODILE!' she shouted, but it came out as 'GNASH GNASH GNASH, GNASH GNASH GNASH-GNASH-GNASH!'

'I'm Ronald,' the mermaid with the official hat said to Jelly. 'New in town, just moved from Octopolli. Did you hear about the Chomp crash?'

Jelly nodded. 'Something fishy is going on. It's not normally like this, you know.'

Paris tried to swim away, but Ronald grabbed her tail. 'Oh sorry, little croc, just a quick trip to Dragonholm Palace and then you can be on your way!'

MARITZA MIST'S
WATER WITCH CATALOGUE

SHELL TALK!

Want to talk to your magic mermaid friends when
they are far away? With this clam compact,
you can see each other and talk for hours!

INSTRUCTIONS: Put some sharpits in the
slot and shout the name of the mermaid
you wish to speak to. They won't need a clam
compact because your face will appear
on the nearest fish.

17

Krilky and the Crabagram Problem

The washing machine spat Beattie out into a grand stone room with a severe pointed ceiling. Around the room, strange tiny boxes and bottles and bags floated about, guarded by angry-looking, equally tiny fish. Gronnyupple flopped out after her and floated alongside Mimi.

Zelda and Steve came tumbling out and straightened themselves up.

'Oh wow,' Zelda said flatly. 'We're so much closer to home.' She tried to grab one of the floating bottles, but the fish guarding it bit her. 'I did not just get sucked tail-first through a washing machine to be bitten by a fish. And *that* is a sentence I never thought I'd say.'

A triangular door rolled up and a mermaid with a cloud of bright blue hair swam in. She looked only a few

 130

years older than Beattie, and wore a crown made of spiked shards of emeralds.

She stopped when she saw Beattie, Mimi and Zelda.

'Found another water witch,' Gronnyupple said, prodding Beattie. 'The others aren't magic.'

'Well, I still don't believe *you're* magic!' Zelda said to Gronnyupple.

'She's not magic but she can do fast things with her fingers,' Gronnyupple said, pointing at Mimi.

Mimi bowed. 'I practise fin-fu.'

The mermaid with the blue hair looked cautiously at Gronnyupple.

'Don't worry, Your Fishiness!' Gronnyupple said. 'They won't tell anyone about us – they're from the Hidden Lagoon. Bet that's a place you've never heard of. Surely I get a bonus for that?'

The mermaid with the blue hair looked intrigued.

'I'm Her Royal Fishiness, Krilky Dragonholm,' she said, turning to Beattie. 'Ruler of the Crocodile Kingdom, leader of the Atlantic realms and secret supporter of water witches.'

'I'm Beattie, mermaid from the Hidden Lagoon and apparently a water witch.'

'I'm Mimi,' Mimi said. 'I do fin-fu and hear things.'

'I'm Zelda,' Zelda said. 'I just got bitten by a fish.'

'AND I AM STEVE,' Steve said grandly. 'I'm a miracle until proven otherwise.'

'He thought he was the only seahorse who could speak,' Gronnyupple whispered to Krilky. 'Then we told him about all the talking seahorses in Pinkly.' She winked.

'I help Krilky with my powers from time to time,' Gronnyupple explained to the others. 'In return, Krilky gives me sharpits to buy things from *Maritza Mist's Water Witch Catalogue*. She's not magic, so she needs me in order to use them.'

'Gronnyupple has told us a lot about the catalogue,' Beattie said. 'And she seems to think I'm also a water witch. But now she's promised she'll help us get back to the Hidden Lagoon. We just want to go home.'

'I understand,' Krilky said. 'But before Gronnyupple helps you, I need her to deal with a more pressing matter.'

'Uh-oh,' Gronnyupple said, shoving Seahorse Surprise sweets into her mouth and staring at Krilky like she was an intense film.

'I have a mission for you, Gronnyupple, and your new friends can join you.' She turned to Beattie, Mimi and Zelda. 'But I must stress that you keep this a secret. This meeting never happened. That goes for the seahorse too. Help me with this and I will make sure you get home.'

'I don't kno–' Zelda began, but before she could finish, a ringing human phone floated past, hitting her on the head. It halted next to Krilky. She picked up the receiver, releasing a little fish that began spitting bubbles. The bubbles floated together to make words.

'We ... have ... checked ... the ... ripple ... levels ... registering ... from ... the ... area ... around ... Craba-gram ... HQ ... as ... requested ... All ... normal ... and ... correct ... No ... suspicious ... activity ... noted ... Next ... step? ... Please ... advise?'

The fish spat out the last of the bubble letters and began panting.

Krilky held the receiver up to her mouth. 'Thank you, Janet. I have a mermaid team looking into it,' she said slowly and clearly. The little fish heaved itself into the phone receiver and Beattie watched as a small bulge appeared in the wire, then swam on through it and out of the window.

'What just happened?' Zelda asked.

'Telephone call,' Krilky said.

Zelda looked at Beattie, who shrugged. They didn't have technology like that in the Hidden Lagoon.

'Strange things are happening in this place,' Krilky said gravely. 'Chomp crashes, fights. And from what I hear, there's always a crabagram at the centre of it. The Chomp accident this morning, for example, was caused

 134

because a crabagram ended up pasted to the left eyeball of the lead crocodile driving the train. It unbalanced the crocodile and he went flying, taking the train carriages with him. Usually a crabagram crab would never be so unprofessional as to rest on a Chomp crocodile's face!'

Krilky paused to look at them solemnly. 'There's something wrong. I thought a mermaid might be tampering with the crabs as they exit from Crabagram HQ. But I fear it's worse – the problem is somewhere *inside* Crabagram HQ. I need you to go there and check it out. You'll need to use magic – mermaids are strictly banned from entering Crabagram HQ. Even me.'

'This actually sounds fun,' Zelda whispered to Beattie.

There was a knock at the door. 'GOT A CROCODILE FOR YOU TO APPROVE, YOUR FISHINESS,' came a jolly voice.

'Quick, hide,' Krilky said.

Beattie looked around the room – there was nothing

in it apart from tiny floating bottles and boxes. There was nowhere to hide!

Krilky looked panicked. 'This is meant to be a secret operation. No one must see you water witches in here!'

18

Fish Eye

There was another knock on the door. 'Your Royal Fishiness, I've got a new crocodile for you to meet – straight off the whale bus! Needs your royal approval!'

'Everyone relax,' Gronnyupple said, sticking out her tongue in concentration and plucking a bottle from in front of Beattie. She sprinkled the gooey contents over them.

There was a bang and they all multiplied.

Gronnyupple tapped her chin. 'Ah, that was the wrong bottle.'

'Argh!' Zelda cried when she saw another Zelda floating next to her.

Mimi's double shook hands with her.

'FISH EYE!' Beattie's double shouted, as

137

Gronnyupple's tried – to her horror – to eat one of her Seahorse Surprise sweets.

The door swung open and Ronald swam inside, lugging Paris the crocodile on his back.

'Oh, I'm terribly sorry,' he said sheepishly. 'I didn't realise you had guests.' He flipped Paris the crocodile over his shoulder and she flopped into the middle of the room.

'FISH EYE!' Beattie's double shouted. 'FISH EYE! FISH EYE! FISH EYE!'

Beattie felt her face getting hot with a mixture of fear and embarrassment.

Gronnyupple grinned. 'We're all identical twins, and we are in a club called –'

'FISH EYE!' Beattie's double shouted.

'– called Fish Eye,' Gronnyupple finished.

'How wonderful!' Ronald said kindly. 'What does your Fish Eye club do?'

'We save …' Gronnyupple said with a gulp '… fish eyes?'

'An important endeavour,' Ronald said, pushing Paris the crocodile forward.

 138

Mimi cocked her head to one side and swam a bit closer. So did her double.

'I approve the crocodile,' Krilky said quickly. 'It is free to swim the waters of the Crocodile Kingdom.'

Ronald paused, picking at a fingernail awkwardly as he tried to find the right words. 'It's just ... I thought there was a whole ceremony. You know, make a fuss of the new crocodiles?'

Krilky smiled. 'We'll make a fuss later. But right now I really need to finish my meeting with the charity that ...'

'Saves fish eyes,' Gronnyupple said grandly, and with a bow. Beattie stifled a giggle.

'Excellent,' Ronald said, blushing a little pink and turning to leave. 'Come on, croc.'

'I'M A GIRL!' Paris shouted. 'I WORK AT AN ICE-CREAM STALL!' though it came out as 'GNA-GNASH GNASH!' She *had* to communicate with her mermaids, so she dug her claws into the side of the door. Without making it too obvious that he was struggling, Ronald tried to pull the crocodile through the door.

'It … doesn't … want … to … budge,' he panted.

'Just leave the crocodile, I'll sort it out later,' Krilky said impatiently.

Ronald hung his head and swam away sadly.

'That's a girl,' Mimi said casually, pointing at the crocodile.

Krilky stared at Mimi. 'A girl crocodile?'

'No,' Mimi said, shaking her head. 'Just a girl.'

'What do you mean, a girl?' Krilky swam up to Beattie, not taking her eyes off Mimi. 'Is your friend … ill?'

'Mimi has only been sick once in her life,' Zelda said. 'She got this horrible rash and then –'

'I'm not sick. She's a girl, not a crocodile,' Mimi repeated.

'YOU CAN HEAR ME?' Paris cried.

Mimi nodded.

'THE NECKLACE!' Paris shouted, launching into a big ramble about how it was magic and stuck in her teeth and she'd already been a shark and all sorts of other things. 'I NEED TO SHAKE IT ONCE TO

MAKE ME A MERMAID. JUST ONCE! Two shakes is for dolphin, five for human, three for jellyfish …'

Mimi inspected the two teeth, and with one swift fin-fu chop knocked out the necklace. Paris grabbed it with her crocodile claw and shook it just the once.

BOOM!

Paris the mermaid was back in the room.

19

Hilma Goes to a Shockey Match

The giant Saltmont Shelladium glowed a blinding green. It was quite the sight, floating and secured in place with some really strong seaweed above downtown Saltmont.

'What do mercats eat? Maybe we could lay some food traps,' Hilma said as they swam into the stadium.

'They eat tiny fish,' Conrad said quietly.

Hilma paused. 'I have no idea where to buy Tiny Fish. What is it? A purée? A foam? An expensive little sweet?'

'No, it's tiny fish,' Conrad repeated, as a trail of tiny fish floated past.

'One, two, three, four, three,' another of the little mermaids said as she counted them.

Hilma soon grew bored of the conversation and

moved on to reading the shockey board. 'According to this, it's the Saltmont Slammers and the Lava Assassins playing today. I hate shockey.'

The Saltmont Slammers were riding crocodiles and the Lava Assassins were on lava waves.

'Why don't their tails melt?' the little girl mermaid with bunches asked.

'I'm afraid if you don't know the answer to that then I can't tell you,' Hilma said, who had no idea herself.

One of the Saltmont Slammer's crocodiles collided with a Lava Assassin swimmer, sending her flying across the stadium and into the stands. The crowd gasped.

'Boring,' Hilma said. 'It reminds me of a mermaid I know called Zelda, who is one of the best shockey players of all time.'

'Wow, you know a mermaid who is the best at shockey?' the enthusiastic one with the basket wheezed.

'Unfortunately,' Hilma said. 'She's got terrible taste and would probably really like your hat.' She took it off her and threw it at a player riding past on a lava wave.

 143

'My hat melted!' the little mermaid wailed.

'You're welcome,' Hilma whispered as she scanned the stadium. 'Nope, don't see a mercat.'

A mermaid dressed as a crocodile swam past.

'OI!' Hilma yelled, grabbing the mermaid's fake crocodile tail. 'SALTMONT SLAMMERS' MASCOT, HAVE YOU SEEN A MERCAT?'

'No,' the mermaid said, wriggling free of Hilma's grasp. 'I've been doing laps of the stadium and haven't seen one. What's it called?'

'Mrs Slippery Pawpaw,' Conrad said.

'It probably swam away because you gave it such a disgusting name,' Hilma said. 'Right, where were you *before* the shockey stadium?'

 144

20

Packing Up Some Magic

'So you can understand sea creatures,' Krilky said. 'You're a Fish Talker. That's very impressive. And potentially useful to me.'

Mimi shrugged. 'I like to talk to everything.'

'Fish Talkers and water witches have been friends for centuries. Fish talking is almost magic – and just as mysterious,' Gronnyupple said. She turned to Zelda. 'You're the only not-remotely-magic one.'

Paris floated with her mouth ajar as Krilky inspected her necklace. She wanted to tell them everything, but the shock of successfully finding the mermaids had rendered her speechless.

'There are things floating in this,' Krilky said, pulling the necklace forwards and Paris with it. Gronnyupple leaned closer and furrowed her brow.

 145

'This is some serious magic,' she said. 'Look, there's a jellyfish, and a dolphin. It's a morphing necklace. They are almost impossible to make – I know Maritza Mist can't make them, because I asked her once. This must've been made a long, long time ago. Can you morph into the things that are floating in here?'

Paris nodded.

'Well, what do you know!' Gronnyupple said with a snort. 'Another water witch! You wait your whole life to meet one and then two come along at once!'

'OK,' Paris said with a meek smile.

'Oh no,' Gronnyupple gasped. 'There's an H-word in the necklace too!'

'Just say "human"!' Zelda said. 'Unless you mean a hairdryer?'

'Oh, I don't know what we'd do if we found a human in our kingdom,' Krilky said. 'I would not want to be that human …'

Paris gulped.

'Where did you get this?' Krilky asked.

Paris's mouth fell open a bit more and one of the tiny

angry fish swam in and out of it. Her mind was racing – if the mermaids hated humans she could hardly say she got it when she was freeing a mermaid on land. Although, freeing a mermaid would make her look good … but then she might have to explain it was her mother who fishnapped the mermaid in the first place. She definitely couldn't tell them she was a human!

'Found it,' she eventually rasped.

'You found it?' Krilky asked, sounding suspicious.

'LUCKY FIND!' Gronnyupple roared, punching the air. 'Can we order things from the catalogue now?'

Krilky pulled Gronnyupple aside and handed her a map. 'This is how to get to Crabagram HQ.' She lowered her voice to a whisper. 'It is crucial that no crab sees you either inside or trying to get in. It's highly illegal, and I can't have it traced back to me. I'm the Royal Fishiness.'

Gronnyupple grunted and began flicking through *Maritza Mist's Water Witch Catalogue*.

'We'll take her too,' Mimi said, linking arms with Paris. 'And then she can come home with us. She's from the same place, aren't you?' Mimi winked.

Paris nodded.

Gronnyupple waved the catalogue in front of Zelda's face.

'Seriously?' Zelda said, grabbing it. 'I could order some magic?'

Gronnyupple nodded. 'You could order it, but you're not a water witch, so you wouldn't be able to use it.'

Zelda's tail wilted.

'Place your order,' Krilky said. 'And then get on with the mission.'

'We'll take … one of everything,' Gronnyupple said. 'This month is a good one.'

Beattie leaned over to take a peek.

'It updates automatically by magic,' Gronnyupple said, running her hand over it.

While the others were busy, Mimi pulled a still bewildered Paris to one side. 'It's all right. I know you're a human. Don't worry, you're safe.'

'Can you hear my thoughts too?' Paris whispered, her eyes wide.

'No, I just heard you shouting about an ice-cream

stall when you were a crocodile, and I remember you from when I was on land. I thought you looked familiar. The tail threw me.'

Paris breathed a sigh of relief and launched herself at Mimi, hugging her tightly. 'Thank you,' she said.

'Well, that latest order won't arrive for a few days, so we'll have to make do with what we have here,' said Gronnyupple. She swam over and began plucking potions and boxes from around the room and stuffing them in Paris's backpack. 'Magic supplies! Magic supplies!' she sang.

'Do you have a magic plan to get us inside Crabagram HQ unnoticed?' Beattie asked hopefully.

Gronnyupple snorted. 'Ha! I *never* have a plan.'

'FISH EYE!' Beattie's double shouted.

'Leave the doubles here,' Krilky said. 'They'll fade soon. Good luck on your mission.'

Gronnyupple bowed. 'Thank you, Your Fishiness.'

Krilky bowed her head. 'Now if you don't mind, I'm going to check the shockey score.' She turned to the wall and pressed a button. A stone screen popped up showing the latest shockey match.

'Bye … Fishiness,' Beattie said as she swam straight past, but she stopped before she reached the door. 'That mermaid at the shockey match looks just like Hilma,' she said.

'Yeah,' Zelda said, dragging Beattie out of the room. 'Because Hilma has swum off the boat and taken herself to a shockey match.'

'You're right,' Beattie said. 'I'm being ridiculous.'

MARITZA MIST'S
WATER WITCH CATALOGUE

TINY-IT!
One drink makes you shrink!

Ever wanted to make yourself the size of a
small rock or even a single grain of sand?
Well, now you can! Tiny-It is a simple sip
potion that can be used to make any
mermaid pocket-sized.

WARNING: In line with Water Witch Council rules,
you must not use this potion more than three times a year,
due to risks of permanent shrinkage.

21

Return of the Clam Car

The five mermaids, and Steve, took one of the secret back entrances out of Dragonholm Palace and emerged in the grand gardens. Gronnyupple swam on ahead. 'We'll need to take the Chomp all the way to Lava. There's Saltmont Station just up here on the edge of the park – next to the coral maze.'

Before they reached it, Beattie saw crowds of mermaids swimming around in an angry-looking clump. A mermaid in an official Chomp cap and with a large crocodile badge on his arm was directing them away.

'CHOMP CLOSED UNTIL FURTHER NOTICE!' Beattie could hear him shouting as they swam closer.

'Closed?' Gronnyupple said. 'That never happens.'

'Why is it closed?' Zelda asked the Chomp mermaid.

'Nothing to be alarmed about,' he said. 'Just a bit of a crashing problem. Travel has been suspended until we're sure the Chomp network is safe.'

'Well, this is a problem,' Gronnyupple said. 'Lava is far away, it'll take us days to swim it.'

Paris tugged at Mimi's arm.

'We need to find my mother,' she said urgently. 'She's an *H-word*. But she's disguised as a mermaid.'

'Oh, that's nice of her. Did she join you for the swim?' Mimi chirped.

'No, no,' Paris said, talking fast. 'She's going to dig this place up and fishnap all the mermaids. She's building a Mermaid World on land and is here to find things to fill it!'

'OK,' Mimi said with a kind smile. 'I'll just tell the others.'

'You can't!' Paris cried. 'You saw how much Krilky and Gronnyupple hate H-words. If we tell them about my mother, they'll know I'm a human.'

'Well, we have this mission to do first, and it seems

very important,' Mimi said. 'Maybe we'll see your mother on the way there.'

'No, you don't understand. My mother, she's troub–'

A mermaid pushed between them before Paris could finish. 'LET ME ON, YOU MENACE!' she shouted at the Chomp mermaid. 'I NEED TO GET ALL THE WAY ACROSS TOWN!'

'CHOMP CLOSED UNTIL FURTHER NOTICE!' he shouted back. 'TAKE THE SWIMWAY!'

Beattie looked to where he was pointing – curving all around the pointed buildings of Saltmont were hundreds of clear pipes, filled with mermaids and streams of bubbles.

'Bubbles make them go faster,' Gronnyupple said when she noticed Beattie looking. 'Unfortunately for us, the swimways just go around Saltmont, not out of town to Lava.'

There was a groaning noise that echoed loudly, causing all the fish and mermaids to stop.

 154

'Uh-oh …' Gronnyupple said, just as Beattie spotted the problem. One of the swimways was packed to bursting with mermaids.

'THE SWIMWAYS CAN'T TAKE THIS MANY OF US!' one of the mermaids in the crowd shouted, swimming fast towards the pipe, just as there was an almighty crack and the pipe exploded, scattering mermaids everywhere.

'Quickly!' someone shouted. 'Get the Cod Bods!'

'Cod Bods?' Paris said.

'The emergency medical mermaids,' Beattie said.

'Oh, like doctors and nurses,' Paris said.

Zelda spun round. 'Wait, how do you know human words?'

Mimi widened her eyes at Zelda to get her to be quiet.

'Curious,' Zelda said, raising her eyebrow.

'What's curious?' Gronnyupple said.

'Oh, um, nothing,' Zelda said, not taking her eyes off Mimi, who was now shaking her head. 'Gronnyupple, don't you have a spell that could get us to Lava?'

'Good idea!' Gronnyupple cried, pulling Paris by the backpack and rifling around inside. 'Ah, I do have some fast forward.' She shook the jar. 'But only enough for one mermaid, and we all need to get there.' She dug a little deeper into Paris's backpack. 'Ah ha! I also have an extra sachet of Floop, only this is a more powerful blend.'

'What does the more powerful blend do?' Beattie dared to ask.

Gronnyupple shrugged. 'Find things better? I don't know. Why don't you try it? Open the sachet, run the gloop through your fingers and think about finding a way to get to Lava. Then hold out your hand and the thing we most need will fall into it!'

Beattie reluctantly ripped the sachet open to the sound of Zelda sniggering.

'I still don't believe this stuff,' Zelda said.

Beattie ran her hand through the gloop and squeezed her eyes shut. She imagined soaring over the spiky rooftops of Saltmont. 'IS ANYTHING HAPPENING?' she shouted.

'Nah,' Zelda said. 'Now if we could just –'

'Just what?' Beattie said. 'Zelda?' She opened her eyes to see them all looking up, their mouths hanging open.

'What is it?' Beattie said slowly, just as a huge clam car fell on to her hand, and the rest of her, with a crunch.

 157

'IT WORKED!' Zelda cried, as a thick cloud of sand and bits of coral mushroomed around them.

Zelda pushed Mimi and Paris out of the way so she could pull Beattie free.

Beattie coughed and spluttered and spat out sand. She felt like she'd just eaten a beach. When the sand cleared, she could see that it wasn't just any old clam car.

'It's our clam car,' Mimi explained to Paris. 'We decorated it back in our lagoon.'

'Unbelievable!' Beattie cried as she swam around it. It was the real thing, with the little doodle of the piranha in the sandwich and everything.

Gronnyupple lifted the lid on the clam car and clambered inside. 'To Lava!'

'We can do this,' Beattie said quietly. 'We have magic on our side.'

'And fin-fu!' Mimi said cheerily. 'And Fish Talking.'

'And morphing,' Paris said, holding up her necklace.

'I'll just drive, shall I?' Zelda said flatly.

THE SQUEAKER

SEAHORSE SURPRISE!

The classic Crocodile Kingdom sweet is back – with a new and improved recipe. A thick, delicious jigglesand shell can be cracked open or sucked for hours, revealing a second surprise sweet inside!

WARNING: Never feed to crocodiles. It gives them too much energy and makes them swim upright or, in extreme cases, belly up.

DON'T FORGET: Auditions to become the face of Seahorse Surprise are happening now. Think you could be the new face? Then swim on down to our factory at Nibblehollow to audition!

22

Crabagram HQ

The first thing Beattie noticed about Lava was the rumbling. The city was built into the rim of a volcano, with hundreds of houses, shops and swimways carved into the rock.

The clam car swirled down past the Redmelt Hotel and a long line of mermaids riding on a wave of lava.

Paris snored loudly in the back, surrounded by the packets of Seahorse Surprise she'd scoffed. Mimi patted her head. 'Poor Paris is exhausted. She's been on quite the adventure.'

'According to Krilky's instructions, the entrance to Crabagram HQ is hidden next to a place called Clawbridge Manor,' Beattie said, as she wiped the steamed-up window and peered out. She could barely see the names of the houses behind the dripping lava.

'Is it just me or is it really hot in here?' Zelda said, turning round in her seat to see steam wafting from Steve.

'THERE IT IS!' Beattie cried. 'Clawbridge Manor!'

Zelda pulled a lever on the clam car, making it screech to a halt.

They watched in silence as a crab scuttled down the rocky street, cradling a crabagram.

'Where did he come from?' Beattie said. 'Did anyone see?'

'Maybe HQ is in the house,' Mimi said.

'No,' Beattie said, pointing at an old sunken postbox next to the house. 'That's it.'

'What *is it*?' Gronnyupple said. 'A red present?'

'It's an old human postbox,' Beattie said. 'They put letters in them.'

'Ah!' Gronnyupple said with a snort. 'It's a joke! Most mermaids wouldn't know that – I would've guessed red presents. Good one, crabs!'

A crab peeped through the slot and then jumped out.

'See,' Beattie said, feeling slightly smug about

figuring it out. Her time on land with legs had definitely been worth it!

'Remember what Krilky said,' Gronnyupple whispered. 'We can't let the crabs see us entering. Only Beattie and I can use magic – if you don't count snoring Paris – so we'll go. You all keep watch.'

'EXCUSE YOU. If Beattie is going in, I am coming too,' Steve said.

'That's very sweet of you, Steve, but I can look after myse–'

'It's because I don't want to stay in the car with Zelda,' Steve said, cutting her off.

'Oh, OK,' Beattie said as she began searching through Paris's backpack. 'What magic should we use?'

Gronnyupple grinned. 'I have just the thing.'

The Tiny-It potion tasted *terrible*, like rotten foam shake, Beattie thought. And the

shrinking didn't
work uniformly all over –
her hair didn't shrink nearly as much as her tail, and
one of her hands remained quite large.

'It's not very good, is it?' she hissed at Gronnyupple.

'No spell is perfect,' Gronnyupple said, with
one eye three times the size of the other.

It was a long drop inside the old sunken
postbox. Beattie, Gronnyupple and Steve swam down
and down, past rock caves covered in scuttling crabs.
They seemed to move in sensible lines, darting in
and out of caves, carrying soggy seaweed crabagrams and parcels. Crabs floated in from every
angle, landing on the rock and joining queues.
Rickety lifts went up and down, carrying
parcels and clumps of crabs to different
floors.

'What are we looking for?' Beattie said
as they reached the very bottom. A crab
barged past, making her jump.

'You don't need to worry!' Gronnyupple said. 'We're so tiny they can't see us. We're practically microscopic! Good old Tiny-It potion. One drink makes you shrink!'

Steve was his regular size, because no crab would worry about a seahorse swimming by. He was nevertheless being cautious and was swimming along the floor flat on his back. Only the cone top he was wearing stuck out.

'And the beauty of being small –' Gronnyupple said with a smile, gesturing towards one of the crabagram crabs passing by – 'is that the words are so big you can read everything clearly … *See*, that one says … *FOR STACEY SL–*'

The crab had already gone.

Gronnyupple chuckled nervously. 'I suppose the downside is the words are so overwhelmingly large, and the crabs are moving so fast it's difficult to read them.' She shot off after the crabagram trying to read it.

'SLOPSIT!' she shouted back to them. 'IT'S FOR A MERMAID CALLED STACEY SLOPSIT.'

Beattie put her tiny head in her tiny hands.

'What are we even looking for?' she said, as a line of crabs walked past, the sound of their scuttling legs was almost deafening.

'*Strange things*,' Gronnyupple said, swimming up to Beattie and whispering in her ear.

'We're all strange,' Steve said.

MEANWHILE, BACK IN THE CLAM CAR ...

Paris jolted awake. 'Eee-eeek!' she shouted.

'Paris is a human,' Mimi said casually, as soon as Gronnyupple was out of sight. 'She thought Gronnyupple might do something to her if she told her.'

'Ah, makes sense!' Zelda said. 'Wait. Do you work at an ice-cream stall?'

Paris rubbed her eyes. 'Yes. Where you did your summer on land with legs.'

'You *knew* about that?' Zelda said. 'I thought no one saw us.'

'Just me,' Paris said proudly. 'Actually, that's the reason I'm here. Because I ... well ... I put some trackers on you, figured out you were in the Crocodile Kingdom, accidentally revealed the location of the Crocodile Kingdom to my mother, who was planning to attack your Hidden Lagoon to stock up her Mermaid World – long story – but has now turned her attention to this kingdom, and, well, she's here and I need to find her and stop her.'

Zelda smiled and patted Paris on the back. 'Don't worry, one human won't be a problem. There are bigger problems in this town at the moment. And Krilky thinks it's got something to do with the crabs.'

'Wait,' Paris said. 'Crab problems?'

'That's why we're here,' Zelda explained. 'Weren't you listening? Krilky thinks the strange things happening around town are something to do with the crabagram crabs, so we're checking it out.'

'I didn't hear anyone talking about crabs!' Paris cried. 'I just knew you were on some royal mission. No one said "crab" to me!'

'I guess most of that conversation happened *before* you barged in as a crocodile,' Zelda said.

'It doesn't matter that you didn't know,' Mimi said sweetly. 'You know now.'

'No, no,' Paris said urgently. 'But I know what the crabagram problem is! It's my mother! Susan Silkensocks! She released millions of crabs into the sea – all over the world. It's just a distraction. A way to cause havoc. Phase one of her plan! We need to find her.'

There was a knock on the window.

'Yep, that spell did not last. The crabs saw me. Lots of them. That was one hundred per cent unsuccessful,' Gronnyupple said. She was floating outside with a crab clipped to her ear, one on to her nose and a few on her tail and fingers. 'More are on the way to nip me. Could you let me in?'

'Where's Beattie?' Zelda shouted out to her.

Gronnyupple pointed to the expanding mermaid trying to claw her way out of the postbox.

Zelda shot out of the clam car and pulled Beattie to safety. An angry crab with a soggy seaweed crabagram had attached itself to her tail. Zelda prised it off and turned it over. There was no official *CRABAGRAM* stamp on the underside of its shell.

'It's not a real crabagram crab,' Zelda said, pulling the soggy crabagram note from its pincers and stuffing it inside her waistcoat. 'Beattie!' she said. 'We need to tie as much seaweed as possible around the postbox!'

'Why?' Beattie asked.

'TO STOP SUSAN SILKENSOCKS'S FAKE CRABAGRAM CRABS FROM GETTING OUT!'

'Huh?' Beattie said, slapping away an angry crab with her tail. 'Who is Susan Silkensocks?'

'I'LL EXPLAIN IN THE CLAM CAR,' Zelda said as she began wrapping the postbox with seaweed at shockey speed.

Beattie helped tie it all in place and they landed back in the clam car with a thump.

Zelda pulled the top down and fired up the engine.

A bunch of pincer-shaped dents appeared in the roof.

'Time to get out of here,' Zelda said.

'Wait!' Beattie cried. 'Where's Steve?'

 168

An unmistakeable scream erupted from somewhere above them.

'THERE HE IS!' Beattie shouted, pointing at a crab carrying a big yellow bag of Seahorse Surprise. 'That crab's got him in its claw!' It scuttled across the roof of Clawbridge Manor and disappeared through one of the cracks in the rock.

'He could be going anywhere,' Beattie said.

'Nah!' Gronnyupple said confidently. 'That's one of the Seahorse Surprise return sacks. You know, for faulty Seahorse Surprise sweets. That crab is going straight to the Schweetie factory in Nibblehollow.'

'Then that's where we need to go,' Beattie said firmly.

'He's a really unfortunate shape,' Gronnyupple said. 'What are the chances of being shaped exactly like a sweet?'

THE SQUEAKER

WHY NOT SWIM OFF FOR A WEEKEND TO LAVA'S NEWLY REVAMPED REDMELT HOTEL?

Squeaker readers will get an exclusive first look. Swim around the gardens with their impressive lava waterfalls, or curl up inside with a copy of the latest *Squeaker* and Lava's famous drink – the Hot Melty.

23

Schweetie

'We could be on our way home, but no –' Zelda said – 'we have to save Steve.'

'That's not very nice, Zelda,' the false teeth said with a snap.

'Very funny, Mimi,' Zelda said, grabbing them from her and shoving them down the side of the seat.

Beattie's eyes were fixed ahead. Paris was in the front seat, doing the same. Only she wasn't looking for the Schweetie factory, she was looking for her mother.

Paris banged her head against the window. If she was her mother, what would she be doing right now? 'We need to find her,' she whispered to Beattie. 'She can do a lot worse than fake crabagram crabs.'

'As soon as we get Steve we'll find your mother and

make sure nothing else goes wrong,' Beattie reassured her.

'Krilky isn't going to like us doing fun things,' Gronnyupple said.

'THIS ISN'T A FUN THING!' Zelda cried.

Gronnyupple fiddled nervously with her tail, then leaned forward and whispered, 'We're going to a sweet factory. It's quite hard to bring up a sweet factory in conversation and convince someone it was *not* fun.'

'We solved her crabagram problem though,' Zelda said. 'Fake crabs! We blocked their exit from Crabagram HQ. We'll let Krilky know, and she can order a clean-up.'

Gronnyupple looked confused. 'How did you figure it out?'

'Um,' Zelda said. They all fell silent. Now wasn't the time to explain to Gronnyupple that Paris was actually a human. She might freak out and the clam car could not contain a panic.

'OH LOOK!' Gronnyupple cheered. 'There it is!'

Nibblehollow was small compared to Saltmont, with little clusters of mermaid houses in the rocks. The

Schweetie factory sat smack bang in the middle, a tall and spindly building covered in glistening gemstones. Smoke was billowing out of the holes up and down its side.

'It's Schweetie, Beattie!' Zelda said, chuckling to herself. She'd been waiting to say that the whole way there.

Inside, Gronnyupple grabbed a handful of display sweets and shoved them in her mouth. Then spat them out when she realised they were fake and made of rock.

'Think I almost broke a tooth,' she said to herself, putting her fist in her mouth and fishing around for it.

The woman at reception, whose name badge said *LOLLY*, looked concerned.

'We're looking for a small seahorse,' Beattie said. 'Goes by the name of Steve. I think he might've been delivered by crabagram.'

'Oh,' Lolly said. '*That* Steve.'

Beattie paused. 'What do you mean, *that* Steve?'

Steve floated back and forth on the studio set, wearing a pair of shell headphones.

'BEATTIE!' he cried. 'I'm only THE NEW FACE OF SEAHORSE SURPRISE! Apparently the usual model, Finella Flopsy, was in the Chomp accident and couldn't make it – so here I am!'

They were filming the advert for Seahorse Surprise. Steve was to be a grumpy seahorse teenager, listening to music on his shell headphones and swimming around his messy bedroom.

They had asked if he would wear something other than his cone top.

He said no.

'All right, Steve,' Lolly said, inspecting the tiny set. 'Let's do a first take. Remember, you sing the Seahorse Surprise jingle, while dancing around your bedroom.'

'My bedroom is my false teeth. And this bedroom looks like a normal mermaid bedroom,' Steve said.

'I know … Someone mentioned your bedroom is a pair of false teeth. But you see, the thing is, we decided the false teeth are perhaps a bit weird. So we made a normal bedroom instead.'

'Excuse you! I want a fake version of my usual bedroom,' Steve said, curling his tail extra tight in protest.

Lolly looked over to the other factory mermaids. They nodded.

'Very well. We'll reconstruct the set and make the bedroom some large false teeth. We can make them out of candyjelly. Hang on …'

'You never told me how you figured out the crabagram problem,' Gronnyupple said, as a mermaid straightened Steve's cone top. 'How did you know to look for fake crabs?'

'We got some more information,' Beattie said. 'But you have to promise not to freak out.'

Gronnyupple scrunched up her face. 'Do I look like the kind of mermaid who freaks out?'

'Paris is a human,' Zelda said, as the music started and Steve cleared his throat. The lights flashed.

Gronnyupple slowly turned to Paris, her tail shaking. 'H-WORD!' she cried, before turning and smacking her head on a particularly large stone Seahorse Surprise, and knocking herself unconscious.

'Well, that went as expected,' Zelda said, chewing on a sweet as Steve began bouncing around the messy false teeth, singing –

> '*Seahorse Surprise!*
> *Seahorse Surprise!*
> *A feast for your eyes!*
> *You gotta buys …*
> *SEAHORSE SURPRISE!*'

There was a set malfunction. The teeth snapped closed.

Everyone gasped.

The teeth popped back open.

Steve turned to the camera, his shell top slightly asquint.

'Talk to the seahorse,' he said confidently.

'CUT!' Lolly cried, clapping madly. 'Oh that was perfect!'

MARITZA MIST'S
WATER WITCH CATALOGUE

KA-POP!

This paste is really something special! It comes
in a huge, black, sparkly tube and when applied
causes the mermaid to become a living magnet.
Everything within sight will stick to you. Very
handy when going on holiday or moving
house. Or apply to small areas to create great
visual effects! Maritza Mist suggests applying
to your tail when swimming near seaweed,
for instant seaweed tail!

Can be pre-activated if required.

24

Hilma at the Redmelt Hotel

'Welcome to the Redmelt,' the mermaid at the reception desk said. 'Is it your first time in Lava?'

Hilma peered out of the hotel window. There was a cluster of houses, all higgledy-piggledy and coated in dripping lava.

'Can I interest you in one of our famous Hot Melty drinks and perhaps a bite to eat? We can get anything delivered here – Ringletti, Saltmont squidgies, Seahorse Surprise sweets, Jellywich?'

The kids floated in a neat row and all chimed, 'Jellywich!'

'One for each of us,' one of them said with a smile. 'That's one, two, three, four, three.'

'FIVE COMES AFTER FOUR,' Hilma snapped. 'And one for me too.'

'And your name?' the mermaid asked Hilma. 'For the order.'

ONE HOUR LATER …

'We're looking for a mercat,' Hilma said as Jellywich oozed out of the gaps in her teeth and dribbled down her chin. 'It goes by the embarrassing name of Mrs Slippery Pawpaw?'

The receptionist shook his head. 'I'm afraid I haven't seen a mercat.' He paused, then coughed.

'Pardon you,' Hilma said.

He coughed again and held out his hand. 'A tip … for ordering the Jellywiches?'

Hilma grabbed one of the brown caps and plonked it on his head. 'You are *so* welcome.'

MARITZA MIST'S
WATER WITCH CATALOGUE

THE FROSTOPIA FREEZE

If there's one thing we mermaids of Frostopia
know, it's how to freeze! This is a drinking
potion – gulp it down and enjoy being suspended
in a glorious block of ice. The ice block will also
show your favourite TV show while you
relax inside it. Simply get a friend to slap the
block of ice to activate it. The volume can be
controlled by moving your eyeballs up or down.

25

Crunch Diner

The mermaids swam out of the Schweetie offices, just as a whale swam into it, smashing the building to pieces.

They stared, bewildered by the carnage.

'That's a demolition whale,' Mimi said. 'And it seems to think it received a crabagram order to knock the building down. Or at least, that's what it's shouting.'

'This is all my fault,' Paris said as she watched Lolly emerge from the rubble.

'At least I'd already filmed the advert,' Steve said.

They all glared at him.

'What?' he said. 'If this kingdom needs anything right now, it's a miracle until-proven-otherwise talking seahorse and a bit of light entertainment.'

Zelda pulled the crabagram from her waistcoat. 'I got this from the fake crabagram crab.'

**UNDER THE NEW LAWS, SOUP SERVED
AT THIS DINER MUST NOW BE STIRRED
BY VENOMOUS FISH – FOR SAFETY.
VENOMOUS FISH HAVE BEEN PROVEN
TO KEEP MERMAIDS HEALTHY.**

'That's nonsense! And what if you actually ate one of the venomous fish?' Gronnyupple said with a shiver. 'That's made-up and dangerous!'

'Imagine if *that* diner got a crabagram like that,' Beattie said, pointing down Crabbie Alley.

'Wait a sockond!' Paris cried as she swam fast down the alleyway. 'I know that diner!'

They all weaved closer – a rusting sign hung above the entrance:

The Crunch Diner

'How could you possibly know it?' Beattie asked.

'The old mermaid couple on the whale bus mentioned this place!' Paris said, eyeing the poster in the cave window.

'The only place in Saltmont that sells fresh

Jellywiches – new deliveries daily,' Beattie said, reading the poster.

Paris tapped the one next to it. It had feet drawn all over it and a simple message:

The Crocodile Kingdom's only source of sunken human food. Try an old red cabbage, or an egg!

'This is it!' Paris cried as she swam for the door. 'My mother will be here! I'm sure she overheard the old couple on the bus, plus she'd be hungry after the journey, and she's far too fussy to eat mermaid food.'

The place was empty, apart from a mermaid behind the counter. He was crying.

Paris stopped dead in her tracks and turned as pale as her tail. 'My mother's *definitely* been here.'

'What?' Beattie said.

'Look at the crying waiter,' she said.

'Mermaids cry,' Zelda said. 'He could be crying about anything.'

 184

'THAT HORRIBLE MONSTER! SHE STOLE ALL MY SUNKEN HUMAN FOOD. IT TOOK ME YEARS TO COLLECT THAT. AND THE POTATO WAS JUST GROWING ITS LEGS!'

Paris sighed. 'She found this place –'

'And then she robbed it,' Zelda finished.

Paris's tail wilted.

'Do you have a phone I could use?' Gronnyupple asked the waiter. 'I need to make an important call about some fake crabs.'

The waiter looked up and wiped his wet nose. 'Oh, yes, of course.'

As Gronnyupple went to call Krilky, Beattie took a seat at the stone bar with the others. A jellyfish floated past, piled high with empty plates.

'I still have one egg left,' the waiter said, cracking it open.

They all watched as it floated away and out the door.

'You're meant to lick it before it leaves,' he said, his voice quivering.

'Don't cry,' Mimi said. 'I actually don't think many

185

mermaids like human sunken food anyway. I'd love a Jellywich.'

The waiter beamed at her. 'Coming right up.'

'So we need to talk about how we're going to get home,' Zelda said. 'Gronnyupple completed her mission for Krilky. They can take it from here. Now she can help us.'

'I CAN HELP WITH ANYTHING,' Gronnyupple said cheerily as she swam back over to them. 'Thanks for letting me make a call,' she added, giving a thumbs up to the waiter.

'Not before we find my mother,' Paris said.

Zelda leaned over the bar and handed the waiter the crabagram. 'This is a freebie – don't listen to any weird messages like this, OK? It's a hoax.'

The waiter read it carefully and then rushed into the back room and closed the door. There was a sploshing sound and soup dribbled out around the door frame.

'He made the venomous soup,' Zelda mouthed to the others. 'Unbelievable.'

'Where would your mum go around here?' Beattie asked Paris.

'I don't know,' she said. 'I know that she wanted to dig things up for her Mermaid World – she needs landmarks, mermaids for tanks. The crabagrams were a distraction, but she's probably well on her way to phase two of her plan. We're one step behind her when we need to be one step ahead.'

They fell silent. The phone started ringing and the waiter answered it.

'Right you are, six Jellywiches for Hilma at the Redmelt coming right up.'

'Did he just say Hilma?' Zelda asked.

Beattie leapt up. 'Wait, Susan Silkensocks is planning to dig things up. The Kingdom is far too huge to fit in her factory at home, so she'll have to be selective. That means we just need to figure out what would appeal to her. What would she go for?'

'Oh I don't know!' Paris said, diving off her stool and swimming around in frustration. 'This is all my fault!' She swam outside and flopped on to a rock.

'Paris!' Beattie said, following her and flopping down next to her. 'It's not your fault your mother

187

is making terrible choices.'

Paris felt the tears streaming down her face. She looked up, as if by doing so they'd dribble back into her eyes.

And then she saw it.

'F,' she said, a smile spreading across her face. 'That F!'

Beattie was staring up at it too. A giant billboard with an ornate F on it. The small print read:

FLUBIÉRE: Stuff for Your Face.

'That F has followed me around my whole childhood!'

'OK, you have completely lost me,' Beattie said. 'That's a mermaid make-up brand.'

'She has a box with that exact F on it. She's obsessed with it – she said a mermaid gave it to her. It means more to her than anything,' Paris rambled. 'She was here earlier, so she would've seen this billboard too. Plus there were promotional pufferfish for Flubiére on the whale bus. Oh how could I be so silly! She must know by now. She couldn't have missed it!'

'So what you're saying is –' Beattie began.

'She'll start by digging up Flubiére,' Paris said confidently. '*That* will be her plan.'

THE SQUEAKER

CHOMP SPECIAL BEHIND-THE-SCENES TOURS

Ever wondered what it's like behind the scenes at the Chomp? Well, now you can spend a morning working on the Chomp trains, exploring the tunnels and learning how we keep the ancient network of Chomps running smoothly.

CANCELLED UNTIL WE GET THE CHOMPS RUNNING SMOOTHLY AGAIN.

26

Flubiére

Flubiére HQ was nestled at the farthest corner of Emerald Cove, the Kingdom's most expensive city. The city was made entirely of emerald stone, and the crocodiles that swam the waters had emerald claws. There was a general DON'T TOUCH THAT! rule in the city, which made it difficult to get around without someone shouting 'DON'T TOUCH THAT!' at you.

They parked the clam car in one of the emerald parking caves and swam out.

'DON'T TOUCH THAT!' a mermaid shouted at Mimi as she leaned against the wall.

A bunch of young mermaids swam past and stopped when they saw Steve.

'YOU'RE THE FACE OF SEAHORSE SURPRISE!'

'Can we have a picture with you *pleeease*? We love you!' one of them said, and he chucked an old human Polaroid camera at Beattie.

Mermaids didn't have cameras, but there were plenty of shops that sold sunken human ones.

Steve bowed gracefully as the mermaids huddled around him.

Beattie snapped a picture. There was a gurgling whirr and out came a photo. It was soggy and smudged.

Steve floated on the spot looking pleased with himself.

Mermaids lazing on flat rectangular emeralds whizzed by, chatting and laughing.

'What are they travelling on?' Beattie asked, her head turning from left to right as she watched them pass by.

'Emerald Quicks,' Gronnyupple said. 'They were invented in Jewelport.' She jumped on to an empty one and pulled Beattie up. The emerald Quick felt warm under her tail.

Mimi, Paris, Zelda and Steve piled on to another one.

 191

'TO FLUBIÉRE!' Gronnyupple shouted, sending the emerald Quick shooting forward.

'Wah!' Beattie screamed, grabbing the sides so she didn't slip off.

'I feel like an insect on an ice rink!' Zelda shouted from behind them. She was flopped on her front, clinging on for dear life.

'What's an *insect*?' Gronnyupple asked. 'And an ice rink?'

'I LOVE YOU, EMERALD QUICKS!' Paris shouted into the watery depths, making them all laugh.

Beattie and Gronnyupple zigzagged though some buildings at speed, disappeared through an emerald window and emerged further on with a bunch of jellyfish stuck to them.

Gronnyupple threw them off one by one, hitting other emerald Quicks as they passed.

'Look,' Paris cried. 'That must be it!'

A towering emerald building decorated with a pair of giant eyes and long green eyelashes glinted up ahead. Thousands of the Flubiére promotional fish whizzed in

and out of it. Huge clusters of bubbles streamed from the many windows, and as a bubble passed her Beattie could see it contained a Flubiére lip-gloss compact.

'It's how they deliver the make-up to customers and shops,' Gronnyupple said, spotting Beattie gawping at it.

Beattie reached out to touch it.

'DON'T TOUCH THAT!' a mermaid shouted.

The bubble burst with a little pop, and the compact began to sink towards the streets below. A frustrated Flubiére fish zoomed down and gobbled it. Then spat it out in a nice fresh bubble.

The emerald Quicks sped up and soon they were at the foot of Flubiére HQ. It smelled a little like burned hair.

They rolled off the emerald Quicks outside the front door. A little Flubiére fish swam up to Gronnyupple and began applying eyeshadow.

'BACK OFF, BUDDY,' she shouted.

'Look! There's Susan Silkensocks. That's my mother,' Paris whispered urgently.

They darted behind the Flubiére tower and peered around the side.

'You were right, Paris,' Beattie said, giving her a low five.

'Pretty impressive fake tail,' Zelda said.

'She looks more like a mermaid than an H-word,' Gronnyupple said. 'You're sure that's her?'

'Of course,' Paris whispered. 'I can spot her a mile off.'

Susan Silkensocks swam up to the building, stopping every so often to inspect parts of it and peer through the little windows. She drew closer to them.

They edged back.

'She mustn't see me,' Paris said, shaking her necklace twice and morphing into a dolphin.

Streams of promotional pufferfish swam around Susan Silkensocks, trying to get past with their deliveries. Their lips were glowing.

'Ooh! The new glow in the dark lip gloss!' Gronnyupple said loudly, but Zelda shushed her.

There was a mermaid floating outside in a Flubiére

T-shirt. She was sipping a takeaway drink and flicking though *Squeaker* magazine.

'Are you on a break?' they heard Susan Silkensocks ask her.

'No, we're closing,' the mermaid replied.

'So in a few minutes everyone will have left the building?'

'Nah,' the mermaid said. 'The pufferfish live in the building. And they don't sleep until midnight.'

'That's in a few hours,' Susan Silkensocks said thoughtfully, before swimming off.

'WRONG!' Gronnyupple shouted in Paris's face. 'She didn't dig it up.'

'She'll be back,' Paris said. 'At midnight. And we have to be ready for her.'

27

Magic Traps

Gronnyupple tipped Paris's backpack upside down and gave it a good shake. Magic bottles and boxes floated out.

'What if someone finds us in here?' Beattie whispered. They had sneaked into the top floor of Flubiére, right between the massive eyes. Beattie didn't like the thought of getting caught. They could be sent to Viperview Prison.

'They won't find us!' Gronnyupple said loudly. 'They've gone home. We'll set the traps, catch Susan Silkensocks, and then we can tell Krilky we did a little extra mission. I'll definitely get some bonus catalogue orders for that!'

Beattie floated over to rest against a stack of Flubiére boxes, plucking one of the bottles out of the air as she went.

'Tiny-It,' she said, reading the label. 'Are we going to shrink Susan Silkensocks?'

Gronnyupple shrugged. 'Depends if the H-word wants us to shrink her mother?'

'Do whatever you need to,' Paris said, reluctantly biting into a Jellywich Mimi offered her. 'Just don't kill her.'

'We're mermaids,' Gronnyupple said, 'not murderers.'

'What do we do until then?' Zelda groaned, deliberately knocking over a pile of Flubiére compacts with her tail.

'We set the trap,' Gronnyupple said. 'We'll make a route that she'll have to follow. We'll do some magic, capture her, and then I will get the glory and catalogue things from Krilky, and you will all get to go home.'

Paris frowned. She wasn't sure she wanted to go home.

The five of them and Steve raced around the empty Flubiére building, swerving to avoid the promotional pufferfish wearing their glow-in-the-dark lip gloss. They planted Ka-Pop potions and Tiny-It bottles as backups, but the star of the show was one of Gronnyupple's most powerful catalogue purchases.

'So let me get this straight,' Beattie said. 'Gronnyupple will hide in this room between the big Flubiére eyes, with the Frostopia Freeze potion ready to go. Steve will lead Susan Silkensocks in here by –'

'Being a miracle,' Steve said, snapping open his false teeth before disappearing inside again.

'And then we'll freeze her,' Beattie went on. 'And then figure out a way to get her back to land. If she gets away, she'll swim into the other potions and spells – and it'll be up to me and Paris to activate them.'

The others nodded.

'Now what?' Paris said.

'I'm going to answer some of my agony aunt letters for the *Squeaker*,' Gronnyupple said, waving a stack of seaweed papers. 'Mimi, you'd be a good agony aunt – why don't you help me?'

'Oh, no thank you,' Mimi said politely. 'I don't like to be in agony.'

Zelda put her head in her hands and groaned.

Mimi thought for a moment. 'And I don't think I'm an aunt.'

'No, Mimi,' Beattie said with a giggle. 'An agony aunt is someone who answers readers' letters! They write in with their problems and then the agony aunt answers them.'

'Oh,' Mimi said. 'I can do that. But I still don't understand what it's got to do with pain and relatives.'

Dear Agony Aunt,

My hair is just horrible. I hate it. It's green, but not a nice bright green, it's a dull swampy one. All my friends have bright green hair.

Please help,

Wendy Scales

Dear Wendy Scales and her hair,

Firstly, your name is excellent. Secondly, I'm sorry you two aren't getting along right now. Wendy, instead of answering your question via a letter from me, I'm going to write the letter as if it is from your hair.

Dear Wendy Scales,

Yes, you are right, I am not bright green but swampy, which makes your hair look different to most of the other mermaids you know. But that only makes us stand out. Also, do you know how hard I work to grow out of your head? It takes a reeeeeally long time and all my effort, and I have no time to play sports or even have any friends. We are a team – an excellent, swampy team, and I am yours and no one else's.

Sincerely,

Your swampy hair (who loves you very much)

Mimi handed the letter to Gronnyupple, who scanned it quickly.

'It's perfect,' she said with a smile. 'And your hand-writing looks exactly like the kind of writing hair would have if it had hands.'

Outside, in the middle of Emerald Cove, a dolphin squeaked midnight.

'So now all we have to do is wait for her,' Zelda said.

They didn't have to wait long.

28

Susan Silkensocks Susan Silkensocks

'I heard something,' Beattie said, making the others jump.

'Was it Gronnyupple eating a Jellywich?' Zelda asked.

'No,' Paris whispered, ducking down under the window. 'It's my mother. She's here!'

Before anyone could say anything, Steve – ever the professional – swam out of the false teeth, nose in the air.

Beattie scrambled to the window and peeked out.

Steve made his way up to Susan Silkensocks.

'Hello,' he whispered.

Her mouth fell open. She tried to grab him. He moved to the left, then the right. He ducked under her, sending her somersaulting forward.

'COME HERE, YOU TALKING THING!' she bellowed.

'Told you she'd love Steve,' Paris said with a smile.

Steve weaved back and forth, up and down, reeling her in.

Paris shook her necklace twice, morphed into a dolphin and made for the door. 'She mustn't see me.'

Beattie held her breath as she saw Steve and Susan Silkensocks getting closer and closer to the window.

'COME HERE, I WON'T HURT YOU!' Susan Silkensocks shouted at Steve in frustration.

'Almost there,' Beattie whispered.

Gronnyupple took the stopper out of the potion bottle.

'One …' Beattie said, 'two … THREE!'

There was a BANG! The pufferfish scattered, and there in the middle of the room floated –

'OH, NOT AGAIN!' Gronnyupple cried.

Two Susan Silkensocks.

'Small lumpy bottle is for the double potion,' Gronnyupple said, smacking her hand to her head. 'I was sure I read the label …'

'I thought it was a freeze spell!' Beattie shouted, as Susan Silkensocks and her double tore out of the room and headed in opposite directions.

'Which one is the real one?' Zelda cried.

'I think the one that went left,' Steve said.

'Really?' Gronnyupple said. 'That's interesting, I was thinking the one that went right.'

'WE DON'T HAVE TIME FOR THIS,' Beattie yelled.

'She was definitely more on the left when we swam in,' Mimi mused. 'So that means –'

'COME ON!' Beattie grabbed her.

Paris the dolphin appeared in the dark corridor and shook her necklace, morphing back into a mermaid. 'What happened?'

'Gronnyupple mixed up the potions again – we made two Susan Silkensocks. And now we don't know which is which!'

There was a bang downstairs, followed by a blubbering, bubbling sound.

'I bet she's gone into the bunk room and woken the promotional pufferfish,' Gronnyupple said.

'What is that?' Beattie asked, but Gronnyupple was already out the door.

Beattie tore down the corridor after Gronnyupple, who shot off to the left and disappeared into a room.

A huge puff of smoke billowed out of it.

'Gronnyupple?' Beattie coughed, fighting her way through the smoke.

'Ha!' Gronnyupple cheered as she watched Susan Silkensocks rolling around with several pufferfish stuck to her. 'Magnet spell. Worth every sharpit.'

'EULCH! GET OFF ME!' Susan Silkensocks cried.

Zelda swam up fast behind them. 'Paris just used the shrink spell on Susan Silkensocks upstairs. She's swimming around in a tiny panic.'

'This is the real one,' Beattie said. 'I think.'

'WE NEED MORE MAGIC!' Gronnyupple roared.

'If anything,' Zelda said, 'the magic is making things *worse*. I'll capture the double.' She swam off.

Beattie and the others swam backwards as Susan Silkensocks angrily pulled at the pufferfish stuck to her and clawed her way towards the door.

'YOU!' she seethed at Beattie. 'I'm going to fishnap you!'

Beattie backed away, her tail shaking. Mimi appeared

behind her, holding a perfectly clear glass bottle.

'THE FREEZE ONE!' Gronnyupple cried, swimming above Mimi's head and grabbing the bottle. She tipped it over Susan Silkensocks and –

BOOM!

'LET ME OUT!' Susan Silkensocks roared from inside a huge block of ice.

'Works every time.' Gronnyupple kissed the bottle.

'Is the bottle frozen to your lips?' Steve asked.

'My moant mo mot mou're malking mamout,' Gronnyupple said.

'We did it!' Beattie cried.

'We should send her home now,' Mimi said.

Gronnyupple swam close to the block of ice and put her ear to it. 'She's saying something,' she whispered. 'Listen.'

Steve leaned against the block of ice. Then Mimi, Paris the dolphin and Beattie did too.

It was very muffled. Beattie stuck a finger in her other ear to hear more clearly.

'It's sounds like … wish pie?' Gronnyupple said.

Beattie felt her tail go cold. 'Fish eye,' she said. 'She's not the real Susan Silkensocks, she's the double!'

Mimi looked up. 'If she's the double, then what about –'

'HELP!' they heard Zelda shout. 'FISHNAP!'

29

Hilma on the Chomp

'Can we catch diseases down here?' Hilma asked as she and the five little mermaids swam into the Chomp tunnel. They were safely positioned in an alcove, which was filled with troughs of seaweed mulch to feed the crocodiles. It smelled like seahorse sick, and the familiarity of it made Hilma slightly miss Beattie and the others, and also made her gag.

'The mercats like the mulch!' one of the little mermaids said, as the whole lot of them wriggled out of the seaweed basket and dived into the stuff.

'Wait. A. Second,' Hilma said, grabbing the edge of the trough and gripping it so hard her knuckles cracked. She rolled her eyes and sighed. 'All the mercats are here.'

'But Conrad's one is missing,' the little mermaid

with the basket said. 'Look – one, two, three, four, three.'

'No,' Hilma said through gritted teeth. 'One, two, three, four, *five*.'

'Oh!' the little mermaid said. 'They've been here all along. We just counted them wrong!'

'Oops,' Conrad said.

'THIS HAS BEEN A COMPLETE WASTE OF MY TIME!' Hilma scoffed. She stared at the only little mermaid still wearing a brown cap. 'Though I have managed to rid you all of the horrible brown hats, which is so brave of me. Give me that last one,' she said, snatching it off the little mermaid's head.

She turned to the trough, readying to give it a good dunk in the seaweed mulch, when –

'Oh, look!' Conrad cheered. 'A REAL LIVE CHOMP TRAIN! And a mermaid is swimming above it!'

Hilma looked up and her mouth fell open. 'BEATTIE?!'

The Chomp train's horn sounded. Lights flashed in the tunnel. Hilma looked down at the brown hat and smirked, before swimming up in the alcove, leaning over and –

30

The Chomp Chase

FIVE MINUTES EARLIER …

The ground beneath Flubiére cracked, knocking over buildings nearby and sending crocodiles spinning in all directions.

Susan Silkensocks laughed as she and Zelda watched the Flubiére building float up past them to the surface. 'Well, those little removal gadgets I stuck to the bottom of the building worked a treat! Thanks for making me small – it was so much easier to do it undetected that way. It lasted the perfect amount of time, and then POP! I was back to my normal self.'

Zelda groaned.

'I've got boats coming to pick everything up soon,' Susan Silkensocks boasted. 'I just said, Look out for the floating buildings! And you, with your flick of hair, shall be my first mermaid on show in Mermaid World.'

Zelda wriggled and tried to get away, but it was no good. Susan Silkensocks had strapped her tightly to her high-tech fake tail.

Down below, Beattie and the others watched in horror as promotional pufferfish spilled out of the tower.

'There's going to be a lot of homeless promotional pufferfish,' Gronnyupple said.

'Nightmare,' Steve said.

Beattie looked up at Susan Silkensocks and clenched her fists.

'YOUR SHRINK SPELL ONLY HELPED HER!' Zelda yelled down at Gronnyupple.

'GIVE MY FRIEND BACK!' Beattie shouted up at Susan Silkensocks.

Paris shook her necklace four times and morphed from a dolphin into a shark. 'Let's do this, Beattie,' she said. But it of course came out as 'GNASH, GNA-GNASH GNASH'.

Beattie raced on ahead of Mimi and Paris, weaving

in and out of the crowds of mermaids who had been woken by the noise and were fleeing Emerald Cove.

Susan Silkensocks looked back and laughed when she saw them coming. 'Oh please,' she scoffed as she ducked into the Emerald Cove Chomp station.

'She's taking Zelda underground!' Beattie cried, diving in after them.

'NO SHARKS ON THE CHOMP!' an angry mermaid shouted as Paris bit her way through the Chomp token treasure chest and charged after Susan Silkensocks.

They swam through the tunnels, Susan's laughter echoing around them.

'LIMITED SERVICE TO SALTMONT TODAY,' a voice boomed. 'EMERGENCY TRAINS VIA NIBBLEHOLLOW. PLEASE BE ADVISED, DUE TO A CRAB PROBLEM, YOU TRAVEL AT YOUR OWN RISK.'

Beattie bounced off a *Chops & Slinky* poster and went tumbling down one of the tunnels, emerging at a platform packed with mermaids trying to escape the chaos in Emerald Cove.

'NIBBLEHOLLOW STATION IN ONE MINUTE FROM PLATFORM FOUR. FAST CHOMP TO NIBBLEHOLLOW.'

Beattie looked through the old stone archways to the other packed platform. Which one would Susan Silkensocks be on? She began weaving through the crowds.

The station rumbled and the Chomp chugged into view.

'Beattie!' Paris cried, as she morphed back into a mermaid. 'Are we getting on this one?'

Mimi hovered over the crowds on platform four as the train for Nibblehollow arrived.

Beattie gulped. She didn't know what to do! She couldn't see Susan Silkensocks or Zelda. How would she know which train she was going to take?

'TRAIN NOW LEAVING PLATFORM FIVE IS THE LAST TRAIN TO SALTMONT STATION. LAST TRAIN TO SALTMONT.'

Beattie pushed past mermaids, knocking newspapers out of hands and spilling foam shakes.

 216

'What do you want to do?' Paris called to her.

Beattie swam the length of the platform, trying to spot Susan Silkensocks inside the train.

The Chomp doors closed.

'NEXT TRAIN TO LEAVE ON PLATFORM FOUR WILL BE THE FAST TRAIN TO NIBBLEHOLLOW.'

Beattie darted to platform four and scanned the crowds. She didn't seem to be there either! She swam back to Paris and Mimi and the three of them watched as the other train sped out of the station.

'She's not on either of them,' Beattie said, just as she spotted something.

Smooshed in the last carriage, between the old lady with her sea cucumber and a group of worried-looking mermaids with *Chops & Slinky* T-shirts –

'THERE!' Beattie cried.

Susan Silkensocks waved triumphantly as she went past.

'SHE'S ON THIS ONE!' Beattie roared, charging after the Chomp.

Paris shook her necklace and morphed into a shark. They shot off in pursuit.

'WE CAN'T LOSE THEM!' Beattie shouted. But she *was* losing them. No mermaid could swim at Chomp speed! She flicked her tail as fast as she could, but it was no good, the distance between her and the Chomp was growing longer. Paris the shark barged past Beattie and shot forward, grabbing the very edge of the Chomp in her teeth. It rattled precariously, making a few teeth ping out.

Beattie and Mimi lunged for Paris's tail and held on tightly as the Chomp thundered through the tunnel.

They veered left and right to avoid being propelled into the lumpy rock walls, swirling around and around in the tunnel. It was like an intense game of shockey.

'You know who would be really good at catching this train with Zelda on it?' Mimi said airily.

'No, who?' Beattie said.

'Zelda.'

'Thanks, Mimi,' Beattie said through gritted teeth.

There was a chomping sound. Beattie spotted

 218

someone up ahead. Someone with a very large hat and shoulder pads.

'Hilma?' Beattie rasped in complete disbelief as the figure swam up higher. Beattie tried to get a better look, but she was going too fast. She shot past and felt something land on her head.

'I THINK HILMA JUST PUT A SMALL BROWN CAP ON MY HEAD!' Beattie cried, ripping it off and batting it away with her tail.

'MAYBE IT WAS A GOOD LUCK HAT,' Mimi said before roaring 'TUUUUUUUUUUURRRRRRRRN!' as they hurtled towards a sharp curve in the tunnel.

But it was too late. The Chomp pinged from Paris's shark teeth, sending her somersaulting into a wall. Beattie panicked and shot upwards, bashed off the top of the tunnel and was whipped sideways between the carriages. She curled into a ball and rolled into a Chomp crocodile's mouth.

'Excellent driving,' she said sheepishly as it spat her out. She tumbled backwards and watched the train speed off.

'Just great,' she grumbled, dusting herself off.

'Another one!' Mimi shouted from up ahead. Beattie turned round to see another Chomp train hurtling towards her, only this was an older model – and it was taller and wonky, with little crabs crawling all over it.

OUT OF SERVICE flashed on the front of it.

There was nowhere to go – either get squashed at the top or squished at the bottom.

Paris the shark flew past her, right at the train!

'DON'T!' Beattie cried. 'YOU'LL HURT YOURSE–'

Paris bit straight through the roof of a carriage.

'Oh,' Beattie said. 'Good idea.' She shot up and climbed on to Paris's back, soaring fast through the tunnel and over the old out of service Chomp.

'OVER THERE!' Mimi cried, dangling from Paris's tail.

Beattie squinted into the dark tunnel – she could just make out the Chomp carriage Susan Silkensocks was in. She patted Paris.

 220

Paris shot forward, jaws wide, and with an almighty crunch ripped the roof cleanly off.

'WOO HOO!' Beattie cried.

Susan Silkensocks began hurriedly making her way through the carriage, elbowing people out of the way. Zelda was still strapped firmly to her fake tail, being batted by stray mermaid bags and big hats.

But Paris was closing in – taking chunks out of each Chomp carriage as she went.

'Sorry. Sorry. Sorry. Sorry,' Beattie whispered down to each carriage. The mermaids stared up at them in silence.

The tunnel opened on to a platform.

'Nibblehollow!' Beattie shouted as the Chomp screeched to a halt in the station, sending mermaids scattering.

Beattie looked around frantically. 'THERE!' she cried, pointing at the opposite platform. 'She's heading for that platform!'

'THAT ONE IS FOR THE CHOMP TO SALTMONT!' cried a familiar voice behind them.

They all turned to see Gronnyupple floating behind them.

Her timing couldn't have been worse. When they turned back round, Susan Silkensocks and Zelda were gone.

'Wait,' Beattie said. 'Where did they go? No train picked them up.'

Paris shook her necklace with her shark teeth and morphed back into a mermaid. 'Did you see where she went, Gronnyupple?'

'No, but I have an idea!' she said, rummaging around in Paris's backpack. She pulled out a tiny green shell. 'This is Shell Talk.'

She opened it up to reveal a little pearly screen.

'All I have to do is put some sharpits in this slot here, shout "SUSAN SILKENSOCKS" and we can communicate with her.'

'She'll be able to hear us?' Beattie asked.

Gronnyupple dropped some sharpits into the slot and handed it to Paris. 'Better than that – she'll be able to see Paris. When you talk into the shell compact, your face appears on the side of the fish nearest to the person you're calling.'

Paris looked concerned. 'She'll be able to … *see* me?'

'Exactly,' Gronnyupple said. 'She'll see you, stop dead in her tracks and start talking. Beattie, Steve and I will swim around and listen out for her voice.'

Paris straightened up and looked into the shell compact. 'Let's do it.'

'SUSAN SILKENSOCKS!' Gronnyupple roared.

Deep inside the Chomp tunnel that led to Saltmont, Paris's face appeared on a large flat fish swimming next to Susan Silkensocks. Her voice echoed throughout the underground Chomp network.

'MOTHER! SOCK! … I mean, STOP!'

225

31

Paris on a Fish

Susan Silkensocks stopped dead in her tracks.

'Paris?' she said, swimming closer to the fish. 'Your face … it's on a fish.'

'MOTHER, LET THE MERMAID GO.'

Zelda tapped her on the shoulder. 'Your daughter's face on a fish has spoken.'

'Paris?' Susan Silkensocks said again, this time prodding the fish.

'Listen,' Zelda said. 'It's time to stop. I appreciate that you are incredibly entrepreneurial – and I admire that. It's been very interesting hearing your plans and ideas for Mermaid World, but we are *living things*, and you seem to have forgotten that. Also, some of us are magic. And *dangerous*.'

Susan Silkensocks raised an eyebrow. 'Are *you* magic?'

Steve came charging through the tunnel. 'Sensitive subject, Susan!' he cried. 'Sensitive subject!'

Beattie, Paris, Mimi and Gronnyupple emerged from the shadows.

'Paris!' Susan Silkensocks cried. 'You've got a mermaid tail too. Did you also sell your kidney so that experimental company would make one for you?'

'Nope,' Paris said. 'I was just nice and befriended a mermaid.'

'The mermaid queen I fishnapped?' she growled.

Paris nodded. 'But really I did it for your own good. You don't want to be a villain. You make socks. Mermaid World might sound fun to you, but imagine if these mermaids kept you in a cage as a human so they could all look at you.'

Susan Silkensocks clenched her fists. 'BUT I WANT MERMAID WORLD!'

A Flubiére pufferfish swam past, looking bewildered.

Beattie grabbed it and tucked it under her arm. 'What if you had something better than mermaids in tanks? What if you had – at the end of your pier – a magnificent shop that sold your favourite thing?'

'How can a shop sell glory?' Susan Silkensocks said. 'Or winning?'

'It can't,' Beattie said, pushing the pufferfish forward. 'But it can sell *Flubiére*.'

Zelda leaned close to Susan Silkensocks.

'Take it or leave it,' Beattie said.

 228

'It's either Flubiére or we hand you over to her Royal Fishiness, Krilky Dragonholm,' Gronnyupple said firmly. 'And don't let the emerald crown fool you – she's tough, and she really likes sending criminals to Viperview.'

32
Party!

Up and down the streets mermaids celebrated, taking big bites out of Jellywiches and drinking foam shakes. The unofficial crabagram crabs had been rounded up, buildings were no longer toppling, and the Chomp network was being mended – it would be back to its glorious gnashing self in no time.

'What I want to know,' Zelda said to Paris as they shared a Jellywich, 'is why do humans wear socks and shoes and not just socks made out of the stuff shoes are made out of?'

Paris burst out laughing.

'So let me get this straight,' Krilky said, a huge, proud smile smacked on her face. 'You stopped the H-word and then, to convince her not to build Mermaid World on land, you said she could sell Flubiére.'

 230

'The only human in the world who will have it!' Zelda said with a wink.

'I'll make sure she gets regular deliveries. Maybe I'll send them by crocodile, so she knows I mean business,' Krilky said.

'It's win-win for everyone,' Beattie said. 'Susan Silkensocks gets to show off to the other humans, and Flubiére gets extra business.'

Krilky finished off her foam shake and rolled back on her tail. 'Well done, water witches,' she said. 'I'm sure there was a way to do it without eating half a Chomp and destroying various buildings, not to mention thoroughly traumatising the crabs at Crabagram HQ, but still, you got the job done.'

Gronnyupple came swimming up in a fluster, stopping momentarily to take a bite out of a Jellywich that was floating past.

'My order didn't arrive,' she said. 'I went to Eggport to pick it up. Nothing. Maritza Mist *never* fails to deliver a water witch catalogue order.'

The floating phone next to Krilky started ringing.

She lifted the receiver and a fish popped out and began spewing bubble words.

'Urgent ... news ... Your ... Fishiness ... Just ... in ... from ... the ... spies ... in ... Fortress Bay ... Humans ... on ... large ... ships ... were ... spotted ... They ... were ... later ... called ... off ... by ... their ... boss ... a ... human ... they ... called ... Susan ... Silkensocks ... While ... they ... didn't ... end ... up ... doing ... anything ... to ... our ... kingdom ... unfortunately ... due ...

to … their … size … and … the … long … pincers …
on … chains … that … they … dragged … under …
their … ships … there … has … been … significant …
damage … done … to … VIPERVIEW PRISON.

'I'm … afraid … to … inform … you … that …
security … was … breached … and … a … number …
of … high … profile … prisoners …
escaped … including … two … of … the …

most … dangerous … mermaids … in … the … world …
They … have … been … alive … for … over … a … thou-
sand … years … and … yet … have … remained …
eleven … years … old … It … is … said … that … they …
are … immortal … and … judging … by … their …
last … sighting … they … are … en … route …
to … Frostopia.'

Gronnyupple began choking on her Jellywich.
'Maritza Mist didn't deliver my order because she's in
trouble.'

'We don't know that,' Beattie said, trying to comfort
her. 'She might be … on holiday.'

'You don't think it's strange that two immortal
mermaids, *clearly water witches*,' Gronnyupple said,
mouthing the 'water witch' bit, 'were last sighted
heading to Frostopia and now Maritza Mist isn't
responding to catalogue orders?'

'Potentially …' Beattie said. 'But strange things
happen all the time. I'm sure it's nothing serious.'

'I have to find her,' Gronnyupple said. 'Just to be
sure. Water witches stick together.'

'No one has ever found Maritza Mist,' Krilky said. 'She's as mysterious as magic itself. And anyway, Frostopia is out of bounds, and has been for a long time.'

Gronnyupple looked over at Beattie's clam car. 'Not to mermaids from the Hidden Lagoon it hasn't. No one, not even the mermaids of Frostopia, knows that the Hidden Lagoon exists. If I was to go there in a clam car from the Hidden Lagoon, they might just let me in.'

'We sort of need that clam car to get home,' Zelda said, shooting Beattie a look.

'You could meet the greatest water witch that has ever lived,' Gronnyupple said, holding on to Beattie's arm. 'A water witch who can *make* magic. She could teach us how to do it. Without her, we'll have no catalogue, no magic. And when you all leave I'll have no friends.'

'I'm your friend,' Krilky said.

'With all due respect, Your Fishiness,' Gronnyupple said with a bow, 'you're not often available.'

 235

Beattie swished her tail back and forth, an adventurous smile cracking on her face.

'Or,' Zelda said, spotting Beattie's face, 'we could go *home*, and watch *Catwalk Prawn* and live like *normal* mermaids again.'

'Well, *I'll* come with you, Gronnyupple,' Paris said. 'It's the summer holidays, and my ice-cream stall and gadget den are at the bottom of the ocean, so I'll have nothing to do.'

Mimi looked from Zelda to the others and back again.

'No, Mimi,' Zelda said. 'As my twin, you have to do the same as me and come home. It's the law.'

'No it isn't!' Beattie said.

'You're not a twin, Beattie. It's secret twin law,' Zelda said.

A bunch of little mermaids lined up next to them, stroking tiny mercats.

'MERCATS!' Paris roared. 'THE DREAM!' She plucked one from the littlest mermaid and cuddled it.

'Who are they?' Zelda asked.

'Oh, they're my kids,' Hilma said, swimming down in front of them. 'I've been sort of looking after them.'

'Someone left you in charge of *children*?' Zelda spluttered. She bent down to check they were OK. 'Hilma, we thought you were on the *Merry Mary*!'

Beattie gave Hilma a hug. She tried to wriggle out of it.

'I'm going to travel to Beluga Town with them,' Hilma said. 'They've promised they'll get me home from there. I'm quite enjoying having people listen intently to everything I say. Plus they said I could get a mercat.'

'Don't listen to anything Hilma says,' Beattie whispered to the little mermaids.

'Hilma,' Zelda said quietly, 'would you rather have your own mercat or have a hat that miaowed?'

'GOODBYE, ZELDA, goodbye ... other weird

mermaids,' Hilma said, glancing at Gronnyupple and Paris. She turned and said to Beattie quietly, 'See you back at home. I'll set up an appointment so you can meet my soon-to-be-famous mercat. He'll be like Steve, only pleasant.'

'I'M EXCESSIVELY PLEASANT!' Steve roared from inside his false teeth, causing one of the front teeth to ping off and float away. His nose appeared in the gap. 'Plus I'm, until proven otherwise, a *miracle*. A half-fish, half-cat is *hardly* a miracle.'

Beattie watched as Hilma swam off, then turned to the others. 'You know what, Gronnyupple? I don't think a little detour to Frostopia would be a bad thing.'

Krilky lowered her voice to a whisper. 'They say the ice walls are higher than any wall you've seen, and beyond them lies the greatest mermaid city ever built. But no one from outside has been allowed in for *years*.'

'We'll get in,' Beattie said, swimming for the clam car.

Steve popped out of his false teeth, wearing a furry cone top. 'Ready!' he cried.

'Oh, fine,' Zelda huffed. 'I'll come too. Maybe they'll have shockey. What sea creatures do you think they ride?'

'Probably killer whales,' Mimi said.

'Definitely coming,' Zelda said, diving into the car.

Gronnyupple wriggled with excitement, spilling Seahorse Surprise sweets everywhere.

Beattie fired up the clam car.

'There's a secret emergency exit behind the Ringletti stall in Eggport. Tell the mermaid behind the counter that I sent you and she'll let you out,' Krilky said.

'There's an exit there?!' Zelda cried. 'We were closer to getting home at the very start!'

Krilky chuckled. 'But just think what would've happened had you left so soon.' She waved goodbye as the clam car rose up. 'Good luck!'

'Frostopia and then home,' Beattie said with a smile. 'It's just a little detour, after all.'

They had no idea just what a detour it would turn out to be …

THE SQUEAKER

NEWS!

Seahorse Surprise has chosen its new face – and it's a talking seahorse, called Sneeze.

Steve scrunched up the article with his tail and threw it out the window. 'Sneeze?!'

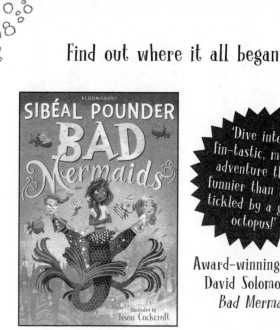

WITCH WARS

Read the whole ritzy, glitzy, witchy series!

AVAILABLE NOW!